GUSTAVE FLAUBERT

A Simple Heart

Translated by
Roger Whitehouse

A Simple Heart

1

For half a century, Madame Aubain's housemaid Félicité was the envy of all the good ladies of Pont-l'Evêque.

For just one hundred francs a year, she did all the cooking and the housework, she saw to the darning, the washing and the ironing, she could bridle a horse, keep the chickens well fed and churn the butter. What is more she remained faithful to her mistress, who, it must be said, was not the easiest of people to get on with.

Madame Aubain had married a handsome but impecunious young man, who had died at the beginning of 1809, leaving her with two very young children and substantial debts. Upon his death, she sold her properties, with the exception of the two farms at Toucques and Geffosses, which between them provided her with an income of no more than five thousand francs in rent, and she moved out of her house in Saint-Melaine to live in another which was less costly to maintain, which had belonged to her family and which was situated behind the market.

This house had a slate roof and stood between an alley

and a narrow street leading down to the river. Inside, the floors were at different levels, making it very easy to trip up. A narrow hallway separated the kitchen from the living room in which Madame Aubain remained all day long, sitting in a wicker armchair close to the casement window. Against the wainscoting, which was painted white, there stood a row of eight mahogany chairs. A barometer hung on the wall above an old piano, piled high with a pyramid-shaped assortment of packets and cardboard boxes. Two easy chairs upholstered in tapestry stood on either side of a Louis-Quinze-style mantelpiece in yellow marble. The clock, in the middle, was designed to look like a Temple of Vesta, and the whole room smelt musty, due to the fact that the floor level was lower than the garden.

On the first floor, there was 'Madame's' bedroom, a very large room, decorated with pale, flowery wallpaper and containing a picture of 'Monsieur' dressed up in the fanciful attire that was fashionable at the time. This room led directly to a smaller bedroom which housed two children's beds, each with the mattress removed. Next came the parlour, which was always kept locked and was full of furniture draped in dust-sheets. Finally, there was a corridor leading to a study; books and papers lay stacked on the shelves of a bookcase which ran around three walls of the room and surrounded a large writing-desk in dark wood. The two end panels of this bookcase were covered in line drawings, landscapes in gouache and etchings by

Audran, a reminder of better days and of more expensive tastes that were now a thing of the past. On the second floor was Félicité's bedroom, lit by a dormer window which looked out over the fields.

Félicité always rose at first light to make sure she was in time for mass, and then worked without a break until the evening. As soon as dinner was finished, the crockery cleared away and the door firmly bolted, she would cover the log fire with ashes and go to sleep in front of the fireplace, holding her rosary in her hand. No one could have been more persistent when it came to haggling over prices and, as for cleanliness, the spotless state of her saucepans was the despair of all the other serving maids in Pont-l'Evêque. She wasted nothing and ate slowly, gathering every crumb of her loaf from the table with her fingers, a twelve-pound loaf baked especially for her and which lasted her twenty days.

In all weathers she wore a printed kerchief fastened behind with a pin, a bonnet which completely covered her hair, grey stockings, a red skirt and over her jacket a bibbed apron like those worn by hospital nurses.

Her face was thin and her voice was shrill. At twenty-five, people took her to be as old as forty. After her fiftieth birthday, it became impossible to say what age she was at all. She hardly ever spoke, and her upright stance and deliberate movements gave her the appearance of a woman made out of wood, driven as if by clockwork.

2

Like other girls, she had once fallen in love.

Her father, a stonemason by trade, had been killed falling from some scaffolding. Following this, her mother died and her sisters went their separate ways. A farmer took her in and, even though she was still a very young girl, he would send her out into the fields to look after the cows. She was dressed in mere rags, she shivered with cold and would lie flat on her stomach to drink water from ponds. She was regularly beaten for no reason at all and was eventually turned out of the house for having stolen thirty sous, a theft of which she was quite innocent. She was taken on at another farm, where she looked after the poultry and, because she was well liked by her employers, her friends were jealous of her.

One evening in August (she was eighteen at the time), she was taken to the village fête at Colleville. She was instantly overcome, bewildered by the boisterous sounds of the fiddle music, the lamps in the trees, the array of brightly coloured clothes, the gold crosses and the lace, all those people moving as one in time to the tune. She was standing on her own, shyly, when a young man, fairly well off to judge by his appearance and who had been leaning against the shaft of a farm wagon smoking his pipe, approached her and asked her to dance. He bought her a glass of cider, a cup of coffee, a cake and a silk scarf

and, imagining that she understood his motive, offered to accompany her back home. As they were walking along the edge of a field of oats, he thrust her to the ground. She was terrified and began to scream. He ran off.

One evening a little later, she was walking along the road leading to Beaumont and was trying to get past a large hay wagon as it lumbered slowly along. As she was edging her way round the wheels, she recognized Théodore.

He looked at her quite unabashed and said she should forgive his behaviour of the other night; he 'had just had too much to drink'.

She did not know how to answer him and wanted to run away.

He immediately began to talk about the harvest and various important people in the district and told her that his father had left Colleville and bought a farm at Les Ecots, which meant that they were now neighbours. 'Oh, are we!' she said. He said that his parents wanted him to settle down but that he was in no rush and preferred to wait until the right woman came along before he married. She lowered her eyes. He then asked her if she was thinking of marrying. She smiled and said that he was wrong to tease her. 'But I am not teasing you, I swear,' he said, and slipped his left arm around her waist. She walked on with his arm still around her. They were now walking more slowly. There was a gentle breeze, the stars were shining, the huge wagon-load of hay swayed from side to side in front of them and dust rose from the feet of the

four horses as they plodded along. Then, without any word of command, the horses turned off to the right. He kissed her once more and she vanished into the darkness.

The following week, Théodore persuaded her to go out with him on several other occasions.

They would meet in a corner of some farmyard, behind a wall or beneath a solitary tree. Félicité was not naive like other young girls of her age; working with the farm animals had taught her a great deal. However, her natural discretion and an intuitive sense of honour prevented her from giving in to Théodore's demands. Théodore found this resistance so frustrating that, in order to satisfy his passion (or maybe out of sheer simple-mindedness), he proposed to her. She was not sure whether to believe him or not, but he insisted that he was serious.

He then announced something rather disturbing: a year ago his parents had paid for someone else to do his military service but he might still be called up at any time. The prospect of serving in the army terrified him. Félicité took this cowardice as a sign of his affection for her and it made her love him all the more. She would slip out of the house at night to meet Théodore, who assailed her with his fears and entreaties.

Eventually, he declared that he would go to the Préfecture himself and find out what the situation was. He would come back and tell Félicité the following Sunday, between eleven o'clock and midnight.

At the appointed time, Félicité ran to meet her lover.

But instead of Théodore, it was one of his friends who stood waiting to meet her.

He informed her that she would never see Théodore again. In order to make sure he could not be called up, he had married a wealthy old lady from Toucques, by the name of Madame Lehoussais.

Félicité's distress was unbounded. She threw herself to the ground, weeping and wailing; she implored God to come to her aid and lay moaning, all alone in the fields, until daylight. Then she made her way back to the farm and announced that she had decided to leave. At the end of the month, having received her wages, she wrapped her few belongings in a shawl and left for Pont-l'Evêque.

Outside the inn she spoke to a woman wearing a widow's hood who, as it happened, was looking for a cook. The young girl knew precious little about cooking but she seemed so willing and so ready to oblige that Madame Aubain eventually said: 'Very well, you may work for me.'

A quarter of an hour later, Félicité was installed in her house.

At first she lived in a constant state of trepidation as a result of 'the sort of house it was' and the memory of 'Monsieur' which seemed to hover over everything! Paul and Virginie, one aged seven and the other barely four, seemed made of some precious material; she liked to give them piggyback rides and was mortified when Madame Aubain instructed her not to keep kissing them. Even so,

she was happy. Her new surroundings were very pleasant and her earlier unhappiness quickly faded.

Every Thursday, a group of Madame Aubain's friends came to play Boston. Félicité would set out the cards and the foot-warmers in readiness. The guests always arrived punctually at eight and left as the clock struck eleven.

On Monday mornings, the secondhand dealer who had a shop at the end of the lane would spread his various bits and pieces of ironmongery out on the pavement. The town would be filled with the buzz of voices, with the sounds of horses neighing, lambs bleating, pigs grunting and carts rattling through the streets. At about midday, just when the market was at its busiest, an old peasant would present himself on Madame Aubain's front doorstep – a tall man with a hooked nose and with his hat perched on the back of his head. This was Robelin, the farmer from Geffosses. He would be followed shortly afterwards by Liébard, the farmer from Toucques, short, fat and red in the face, wearing a grey jacket and leather gaiters complete with spurs.

They would both come bearing chickens or cheeses which they hoped they might persuade their landlady to buy. But Félicité was more than a match for their banter and they always respected her for this.

Madame Aubain also received sporadic visits from the Marquis de Grémanville, an uncle of hers who had squandered his money in loose living and who now lived at Falaise on the last bit of property he could still call his own. He would always turn up at lunch time with a

loathsome little poodle which left its muddy paw marks all over the furniture. Despite his efforts to behave like a gentleman, raising his hat every time he mentioned his 'late father', habit would soon get the better of him and he would pour himself glass after glass and start telling bawdy jokes. Félicité would politely show him to the door. 'I think you have had enough for today, Monsieur de Grémanville! Do come and see us again soon!' And she would close the door behind him.

But she was always delighted to welcome Monsieur Bourais, a retired solicitor. His white cravat and bald head, the flounces on his shirt-front and the generous cut of his brown frock-coat, the special way he had of bending his arm when taking snuff, indeed everything about his person prompted in Félicité the sort of agitation we always feel when in the presence of some great man.

He looked after the management of 'Madame's' properties and would shut himself away with her for hours on end in 'Monsieur's' study. He lived in constant fear for his own reputation, had an inordinate respect for the judiciary and claimed to know some Latin.

Thinking that it would help the children to derive some enjoyment from their studies, he bought them an illustrated geography book. It depicted scenes from different parts of the world, cannibals wearing feathered head-dresses, a monkey abducting a young girl, a group of Bedouins in the desert, a whale being harpooned, and so on.

Paul carefully explained all these pictures to Félicité.

In fact, this was the only time anyone ever taught her how to read a book.

The children received their lessons from Guyot, a rather pitiful character who worked at the Town Hall, who was noted for his fine handwriting and who used to sharpen his penknife on the sole of his shoe.

Whenever the weather was fine, the whole family would get up early and spend the day at the farm at Geffosses.

The farmyard there was on a slope, with the farmhouse in the middle. One could just see the sea, a little streak of grey in the distance.

Félicité would take a few slices of cold meat from her basket and they would eat in a room adjoining the dairy. This room was all that now remained of a country house which had fallen into ruin. The paper hung in strips from the wall and fluttered in the draught. Madame Aubain sat with her head bowed, absorbed in her memories, the children hardly daring to speak. 'Off you go and play,' she would say. And off they went.

Paul would climb up into the barn, catch birds, play ducks and drakes on the pond or bang the great farm barrels with a stick to make them boom like drums.

Virginie would go and feed the rabbits or run off across the fields gathering cornflowers, showing her dainty embroidered knickers as she ran.

One evening in autumn, they were coming back through the fields.

The moon, which was in its first quarter, lit up part of the sky, and a mist drifted like a scarf over the windings of the river Toucques. A group of cattle, lying in the middle of a field, lazily watched them go by. When they came to the third field, a few of them got to their feet and stood in a circle in front of them. 'There's nothing to be frightened of!' said Félicité and, humming a wistful little tune as she approached, she went up to the nearest of the animals and patted it on the back. It turned away and the others did the same. But no sooner had they got through the next field when they heard a terrifying bellowing. It was a bull that had been hidden by the mist. It began to come towards the two women. Madame Aubain wanted to run. 'No, no, we must not move too quickly!' said Félicité. They walked more quickly, even so, and could hear the bull's loud breathing getting nearer behind them and the pounding of its hoofs on the grass. They knew it was now galloping towards them! Félicité turned round to face it, grabbed clods of earth from the ground and flung them into the bull's face. It lowered its muzzle, shook its horns and began to shudder and bellow with rage. Madame Aubain had now reached the edge of the field with the two children and was frantically trying to find a way of getting over the hedge. Félicité was still steadily retreating before the bull, throwing lumps of turf into its eyes and calling out, 'Hurry up! Hurry up!'

Madame Aubain got down into the ditch, pushing first Virginie and then Paul in front of her. She fell several

times as she tried to climb the bank and at last, by dint of sheer determination, she succeeded.

The bull had driven Félicité up against a gate and was blowing slaver into her face. A second later and it would have gored her. In the nick of time she managed to squeeze herself between two bars in the gate. The huge animal was taken completely by surprise and stopped in its tracks.

People in Pont-l'Evêque talked about this adventure for years afterwards. But Félicité never boasted about it and hardly seemed to realize that she had done anything heroic.

Virginie commanded all her attention. The frightening experience with the bull had affected her nerves and Monsieur Poupart, the doctor, recommended sea bathing at Trouville.

In those days, very few people visited the resort. Madame Aubain made enquiries, sought the advice of Bourais and made preparations as if for a long journey.

The day before they left, the luggage was sent off in Liébard's farm wagon. The next day he returned with two horses. One of them had a woman's saddle with a velvet backrest and the other had a cloak rolled up across its back as a makeshift seat. Madame Aubain sat on this behind Liébard. Félicité looked after Virginie on the other horse and Paul rode separately on Monsieur Lechaptois's donkey, which had been lent on the clear understanding that they took great care of it.

The road was so bad that the five-mile journey took them two hours. The horses sank up to their pasterns in

the mud and lurched forward in order to pull themselves free. They lost their footing in the ruts and sometimes had to jump. At certain points on the road, Liébard's mare would suddenly stop dead. Liébard would wait patiently for her to move forward again. As they rode on, he would tell them stories about the people who lived along the way, always adding a few personal comments of his own for good measure. In the town centre of Toucques, for instance, as they were passing alongside a house with nasturtiums growing around the windows, he said, with a shrug of his shoulders, 'There's a Madame Lehoussais lives there and, rather than take a young man . . .' Félicité did not hear the rest, for the horses had broken into a trot and the donkey had run on ahead. They turned down a track, a gate swung open, two young farmhands appeared and they all dismounted beside the manure-heap right outside the front door of the farmhouse.

Old Madame Liébard greeted her mistress with effusive expressions of delight. For lunch she served a sirloin of beef, along with tripe, black pudding, a fricassee of chicken, sparkling cider, a fruit tart and plums in brandy, all accompanied by a stream of compliments to Madame who seemed 'in much better health', to Mademoiselle who had grown up into such 'a fine looking young woman', to Monsieur Paul who was such a 'strapping' young man, not forgetting their dear departed grandparents whom the Liébards had known personally, having been in service to the family for several generations. The farm, like the Liébards themselves,

had an old-world feel to it. The beams in the ceiling were pitted with woodworm, the walls blackened with smoke, the window panes grey with dust. There was an oak dresser, cluttered with all manner of implements – jugs, plates, pewter bowls, wolf-traps, shears for the sheep and a huge syringe which particularly amused the children. In the three yards outside, there was not a single tree which did not have mushrooms growing at its foot or clumps of mistletoe in its branches. Several had been blown down by the wind but had begun to grow again where the trunk had been split and all of them were bent beneath the weight of apples. The thatched roofs looked like brown velvet of unequal thickness and weathered the fiercest winds. But the shed for the carts was falling down. Madame Aubain said that she would arrange to have it repaired and asked for the horses to be reharnessed.

It took them another half-hour to reach Trouville. The little caravan had to dismount when they came to the Ecores, a cliff which jutted out over the boats below. Three minutes later they had arrived at the end of the quay and turned into the courtyard of the Golden Lamb, an inn run by old Madame David.

Virginie very quickly began to recover her strength as a result of the change of air and of bathing in the sea. She did not have a bathing costume and so she went into the water wearing a chemise. Afterwards, her maid would help her to get dressed in a customs officer's hut that was also used by the bathers.

In the afternoon, they would take the donkey and walk out beyond the Roches-Noires, towards Hennequeville. At first the path wound up between gently rolling meadows like the lawn in a park and then came to a plateau where there were grazing pastures and ploughed fields. The path was lined by holly bushes which grew amongst the tangles of brambles, and here and there the branches of a large dead tree traced their zigzag patterns against the blue of the sky.

There was one particular field in which they usually stopped to rest themselves, looking down towards Deauville to their left, Le Havre to their right and, in front of them, the open sea. It lay shimmering in the sunshine, as smooth as the surface of a mirror and so calm that they could barely hear the murmur of the waves. Sparrows twittered from somewhere nearby and the great dome of the sky lay spread out above them. Madame Aubain would sit with her needlework, Virginie would sit beside her, plaiting rushes, Félicité gathered bunches of wild lavender and Paul, utterly bored, would always be itching to move on.

At other times they would take the ferry across the Toucques and go looking for shells. At low tide, sea urchins, ormers and jellyfish were left behind on the sand. The children would chase after flecks of foam blown about by the breeze. The waves broke lazily on the sand from one end of the beach to the other. The beach stretched as far as the eye could see but was bounded on the landward side by sand dunes which separated it from the Marais, a broad

meadow in the shape of a racecourse. As they walked back through it towards Trouville, which lay at the foot of the hill, the town appeared to grow bigger at every step they took and, with its motley assortment of houses, it seemed to blossom like a flower garden in colourful disarray.

When it was too hot, they kept to their room. The dazzling brightness outside cast bars of light through the slats in the window blinds. There was not a sound to be heard in the village. Not a soul ventured out into the streets. The prevailing quiet made everything seem all the more peaceful. From far away came the sound of the caulkers' hammers beating against the hull of a boat and the smell of tar was wafted to them on the listless breeze.

The most exciting event of the day was when the fishing boats came in. Once past the entrance buoys, they would begin to tack from side to side. Their main sails would be lowered to half-mast and, with their foresail swollen like a great balloon, they would come gliding through the splashing waves right into the middle of the harbour and suddenly drop anchor. The boat would then be brought alongside the quay. The sailors would hoist their fish ashore, still live and quivering. A line of carts was ready waiting and women in cotton bonnets rushed forward to take the baskets and to kiss their menfolk.

One day one of these women came up to Félicité. A moment or two later, Félicité was back in the room at the inn, beside herself with excitement. She had found one

of her lost sisters, and into the room walked Nastasie Barette, now Leroux, with a baby at her breast, another child holding her right hand and, on her left, a little ship's boy with his hands on his hips and his beret over one ear.

After a quarter of an hour, Madame Aubain asked her to leave.

But after that there was no getting away from them. They would wait just outside the kitchen or follow them when they went for walks. The husband always kept well out of sight.

Félicité became very attached to them. She bought them a blanket, some shirts and a cooking stove. They were obviously out to take advantage of her. Madame Aubain was annoyed that Félicité was not more firm with them. She also took objection to the familiar way in which the nephew spoke to Paul. So, because Virginie had developed a cough and the weather had taken a turn for the worse, she returned to Pont-l'Evêque.

Monsieur Bourais offered his advice on choosing a good school for Paul. The one at Caen was generally considered to be the best. So Paul was sent away to Caen. He said his goodbyes bravely, really quite pleased that he was going to live somewhere where he would have some friends of his own.

Madame Aubain resigned herself to her son going away, knowing that he must have a good education. Virginie quickly got used to being on her own, but Félicité

found the house very quiet without him. Soon, however, she had something else to occupy her mind. From Christmas onwards she had to take Virginie to catechism every day.

3

Genuflecting as she went in through the door, Félicité walked up the aisle beneath the high ceiling of the nave, opened the door of Madame Aubain's pew, sat herself down and looked all around her.

The children were seated in the choir stalls, the boys on the right and the girls on the left. The priest stood in front of them beside the lectern. One of the stained-glass windows in the apse showed the Holy Spirit looking down on the Virgin Mary. In another, the Virgin knelt before the infant Jesus and behind the tabernacle there was a carving in wood representing Saint Michael slaying the dragon.

The priest began with a summary of the Holy Scriptures. Félicité's mind was filled with images of Paradise, the Flood, the Tower of Babel, cities consumed by flames, peoples dying and idols cast down. This dazzling recital of events instilled in her a wholesome respect for the Almighty and a profound fear of his wrath. She wept at the story of Christ's Passion. Why had they crucified a man who was so kind to children, fed the hungry, gave sight to the blind, and who had chosen, out of his own

gentle nature, to be born amongst the poor on the rough straw of a stable? Seed-time and harvest, the fruits of the vine, all those familiar things mentioned in the gospels had their place in her life too. They now seemed sanctified by contact with God. Félicité loved lambs all the more because of her love for the Lamb of God, and doves now reminded her of the Holy Spirit.

She found it difficult to imagine what the Holy Spirit actually looked like because he was not only a bird but sometimes a fire and sometimes a breath. Perhaps it was the light of the Holy Spirit that she would see at night-time, flickering at the edge of the marshes, or his breath which drove the clouds across the sky, or his voice which made the church bells ring so beautifully. She sat rapt in adoration of these wonders, delighting in the coolness of the stone walls and the peacefulness of the church.

Of church dogma she understood not a word and did not even attempt to understand it. As the curé stood explaining it all to the children and the children repeated what they had learnt, Félicité would drop off to sleep, to be woken suddenly by the clatter of wooden shoes on the stone floor as the children left the church. And so Félicité came to learn her catechism by dint of hearing the children recite it, for her own religious education had been neglected when she was young. From then on, she copied the religious observances of Virginie, fasting when she fasted and going to confession whenever she did. For the feast of Corpus Christi, Félicité and Virginie made an altar of repose together.

For days beforehand, Félicité fretted over the preparations for Virginie's first communion. She worried about her shoes, her rosary, her missal and her gloves. Her hands trembled as she helped Madame Aubain to dress her.

All through the mass she was on tenterhooks. One half of the choir stalls was hidden from her sight by Monsieur Bourais, but straight in front of her she could see the flock of young girls all wearing white crowns over their lowered veils and looking like a field of snow. Even from a distance, she could recognize her beloved little Virginie by the delicate line of her neck and her attitude of reverent contemplation. The bell tinkled. They all bowed their heads and knelt in silence. Then, with a mighty flourish from the organ, the choir and congregation sang the *Agnus Dei*. After the boys had processed forwards, the girls stood up. With their hands joined in prayer, they moved slowly towards the candle-lit altar, knelt at the altar-step, received the Host one by one and returned in the same order to their place in the choir stalls. When it came to Virginie's turn, Félicité leant further forwards so that she could see her and, with that singular imagination that is born of true love, she felt she was herself Virginie, assuming her expression, wearing her dress and with her heart beating inside her breast. As Virginie opened her mouth, Félicité closed her eyes and almost fainted.

The next morning, bright and early, Félicité went to the sacristy and asked to be given communion. She

received it with due reverence but did not experience the same rapture.

Madame Aubain wanted the best possible education for her daughter and, because Guyot was unable to teach her either English or music, she resolved to send her to the Ursuline convent school in Honfleur.

Virginie had no objection to this plan but Félicité was most unhappy and felt that Madame was being too strict. However, she came to accept that it was not really for her to decide and that her mistress probably knew best.

Then one day, an old carriage drew up outside the door. Out of it got a nun who had come to collect Mademoiselle. Félicité loaded the luggage up on to the rack, issued some parting instructions to the driver and put six pots of jam, a dozen pears and a bunch of violets in the boot.

Just as they were about to leave, Virginie burst into tears. She clung to her mother, who kissed her on the forehead and kept telling her: 'Come, come, we must be brave!' The step was pulled up and the carriage drove away.

When it had gone, Madame Aubain broke down and that evening all her friends, Monsieur and Madame Lormeau, Madame Lechaptois, the two Rochefeuille sisters, Monsieur de Houppeville and Bourais, came round to comfort her.

At first, the loss of her daughter left her feeling very sad. But she received letters from her on three days each week

and on the other days she wrote back to her, walked in her garden, read a little and so managed to occupy her time.

Every morning, out of habit, Félicité would go into Virginie's bedroom and gaze at the walls. She missed being able to comb her hair for her, tie her bootlaces and tuck her up in bed; she missed seeing her sweet little face always beside her and holding her hand when they went out for walks. For want of something to do, she tried to take up lace work. But she was too clumsy with her fingers and she kept breaking the threads. She could not put her mind to anything and was losing sleep. She was, in her own words, 'all empty inside'.

In order to provide herself with 'a bit of company', she asked Madame Aubain if her nephew Victor might be allowed to visit her.

He would always arrive on Sundays, just after mass, rosy-cheeked, his shirt unbuttoned and bringing with him the smells of the countryside through which he had travelled. She straight away laid the table for him. They would eat lunch sitting opposite each other, Félicité taking care to eat as little as possible so as to save on expense and giving Victor so much to eat that he ended up falling asleep. As the first bell for vespers began to ring, she would wake him up, give his trousers a good brush, tie his tie, and make her way to church, leaning on his arm like a proud mother.

His parents always told him to make sure he brought something back with him, a bag of sugar, a piece of soap, a little brandy or even money. He brought with him any

of his clothes that needed mending and Félicité always did the work willingly, glad of any opportunity of encouraging him to visit her again.

In August, Victor went to join his father on his sea trips along the coast.

It was the beginning of the school holidays and it was some consolation to Félicité to have the children back at home. But Paul had become rather temperamental and Virginie was now too grown-up to be treated as a little child, which created a sense of awkwardness and distance between them.

Victor's travels took him to Morlaix, to Dunkirk and to Brighton and after each trip he brought back a present for Félicité. The first was a little box made out of shells, the second a coffee cup and the third a big gingerbread man. He was growing into a handsome young man, with a fine figure, the first signs of a moustache, a frank and open expression and a little leather cap which he wore perched on the back of his head like a sea pilot. He would entertain Félicité by telling her stories laced with all sorts of nautical jargon.

One Monday, 14 July 1819 (it was a date that Félicité was never to forget), Victor announced that he had been signed on to the crew of an ocean-going ship and that in two days' time he would be taking the night ferry from Honfleur to join his schooner, which was due shortly to set sail from Le Havre. He might be away for two years.

The prospect of such a long separation left Félicité

feeling very saddened. In order to say one final farewell to him, on the Wednesday evening, after Madame had finished her dinner, she put on her clogs and ran the ten miles from Pont-l'Evêque to Honfleur.

When she came to the Calvary, instead of turning left, she turned right, got lost in the shipyards and had to retrace her steps. She asked directions from some passers-by, who told her she would have to hurry. She walked all the way round the harbour, which was full of boats, getting caught up in the moorings as she went. Suddenly the ground seemed to fall away beneath her, beams of light criss-crossed before her eyes and she thought she must be losing her senses when she saw some horses in the sky overhead.

On the quayside, more horses were neighing, frightened by the sea. They were being hoisted into the air by a derrick and then lowered into a boat which was already crammed with passengers trying to squeeze their way between barrels of cider, baskets of cheese and sacks of grain. Hens were cackling and the captain was swearing. One of the deck-hands, apparently oblivious to everything around him, stood leaning against the cat-head. Félicité had not recognized him and was calling out 'Victor!' again and again. He looked up and she rushed forward, but just at that moment the gangway was suddenly pulled ashore.

The boat moved out of the harbour, hauled along by a group of women who sang in chorus as they went about their work. Its ribs creaked and heavy waves lashed its

bows. The sail swung round and hid everyone from view. The surface of the sea shone like silver in the moonlight and on it the ship appeared as a black spot, growing paler as it moved away. Eventually it was swallowed up in the distance and vanished from sight.

Returning home, Félicité passed by the Calvary and was taken by a sudden desire to commend to God's mercy all that she held dear. She stood there praying for a long time, with tears running down her cheeks and her eyes fixed on the clouds above. The town was fast asleep; the only people about were the customs men. Water could be heard gushing through the holes in the lock-gate like a running torrent. A clock struck two.

The convent would not be open to visitors before daybreak and Félicité knew that, if she arrived back late, Madame was sure to be annoyed. So, although she would have loved just one small kiss from Virginie, she set off back home. The maids at the inn were just waking up as she walked into Pont-l'Evêque.

So poor little Victor was to spend months on end being tossed around on the waves! His previous trips at sea had not bothered her. England and Brittany were places one came back from. But America, the colonies and the Antilles were lost in some unknown region on the other side of the world.

From the day he left, Félicité could not stop thinking about her nephew. When it was hot and sunny, she worried that he might be thirsty and when there was a storm,

she feared he might be struck by lightning. As she listened to the wind howling in the chimney and blowing slates off the roof, she pictured him buffered by the same storm, clinging to the top of a broken mast and being flung backwards into a sheet of foam. At other times, prompted by her recollection of the pictures in the geography book, she imagined him being eaten by savages, captured by monkeys in a forest or dying on some deserted beach. But she never spoke about these worries to anyone.

Madame Aubain had worries of her own about her daughter.

The sisters at the convent said that she was an affectionate child, but over-sensitive. The slightest emotion unsettled her and she had to give up playing the piano.

Her mother insisted that she wrote home regularly. One morning, when the postman had failed to appear, she could scarcely contain her impatience and kept pacing backwards and forwards in her room between her armchair and the window. This really was extraordinary! No news for four days!

Thinking that her own situation might serve as some comfort to her mistress, Félicité ventured:

'But Madame, I haven't received any news for six months!'

'News from whom?'

'Why, news from my nephew,' Félicité gently replied.

'Oh, your nephew!' And with a shrug of her shoulders, Madame Aubain began pacing about the room again, as

if to say, 'I hadn't given him a thought! And in any case, he's no concern of mine! A mere ship's boy, a scrounger; he's not worth bothering about! But someone like my daughter . . . Really!'

Although Félicité had been fed such rough treatment since she was a child, she felt very offended by Madame Aubain. But she soon got over it.

After all, it was to be expected that Madame should get upset about her own daughter.

For Félicité, the two children were of equal importance; they were bound together by her love for them and it seemed right that they should share the same fate.

Félicité learnt from the chemist that Victor's ship had arrived in Havana. He had read the announcement in a newspaper.

Because of its association with cigars, Félicité imagined Havana to be a place in which the only thing people did was to smoke and she pictured Victor walking amongst crowds of Negroes in a cloud of tobacco smoke. Was it possible to return from Havana by land, 'if need be'? How far was it from Pont-l'Evêque? In order to find out, she went to consult Monsieur Bourais.

He reached for his atlas and launched into a disquisition on lines of longitude. Félicité was utterly bewildered. Bourais sat in front of her, beaming smugly to himself, like the know-all he was. Eventually, he picked up his pencil and pointed to an almost invisible black dot in one of the little indentations in the contour of an oval-shaped

patch on the map. 'Here it is,' he said. Félicité peered closely at the map. The network of coloured lines was a strain on her eyes, but it told her nothing. Bourais asked her what was puzzling her and she asked him if he would show her the house in which Victor was living. Bourais raised his arms in the air, sneezed and roared with laughter, delighted to come across someone so simple-minded. Félicité, whose understanding was so limited that she probably even expected to see a picture of her nephew, could not understand what he found so funny.

It was a fortnight after this, at his usual time on market day, that Liébard came into the kitchen and handed Félicité a letter which he had received from her brother-in-law. As neither of them could read, Félicité showed the letter to her mistress.

Madame Aubain, who was counting the stitches on a piece of knitting, put her work to one side, opened the letter, gave a sudden start and then, lowering her voice and looking very serious, she said, 'They are sending you . . . bad news. Your nephew . . .'

Victor was dead. That was all the letter said.

Félicité sank down on to a chair and leant her head against the wall. Her eyelids closed and suddenly flushed pink. She remained there, her head bowed, her hands hanging limply at her side, staring in front of her and repeating over and over again, 'The poor boy! The poor boy!'

Liébard stood looking at her and sighing. Madame Aubain was shaking slightly.

She suggested that Félicité might go and see her sister at Trouville.

Félicité gave a wave of her hand to indicate that it was not necessary.

There was a silence. Old Liébard thought it best to leave.

When he had gone, Félicité said, 'It doesn't matter a bit, not to them it doesn't.'

She lowered her head again and sat there, now and then toying distractedly with the knitting needles that lay on the work-table.

A group of women passed by in the yard, wheeling a barrow-load of dripping linen.

Félicité caught sight of them through the window and suddenly remembered that she had washing to do herself. She had passed the lye through it the day before and today it needed rinsing. She got up and left the room.

Her washing board and her tub were on the bank of the Toucques. She flung her pile of chemises on to the ground beside the river, rolled up her sleeves and seized her battledore. The drubbing could be heard in all the neighbouring gardens. The fields lay deserted and the wind rippled the surface of the river. On the river-bed, long strands of weed drifted with the current, like the hair of corpses floating downstream in the water. Félicité managed to restrain her grief and was very brave until the evening, but when she was alone in her room she gave in to it, lying prone on her mattress with her face buried in the pillow and pressing her fists to her temples.

Much later, she came to learn the circumstances of Victor's death from the captain of his ship. He had caught yellow fever and had been bled too much in the hospital. Four separate doctors had given him the same treatment and he had died immediately. The chief doctor's comment was, 'Good, that's one more to add to the list!'

Victor had always been treated cruelly by his parents and Félicité preferred not to see them again. They did not get in touch with Félicité either; perhaps they had simply forgotten about her or perhaps poverty had hardened their hearts.

Virginie was now growing weaker.

Difficulty in breathing, a persistent cough, a constant high temperature and pale blotches on her cheeks all pointed to some underlying disorder. Monsieur Poupart had advised a holiday in Provence. Madame Aubain decided to follow his advice and would have brought Virginie back home immediately, had it not been for the weather at Pont-l'Evêque.

She had a standing arrangement with a job-master, who drove her to the convent every Tuesday. In the convent garden there was a terrace overlooking the Seine where Virginie would walk up and down over the fallen vine leaves, leaning on her mother's arm. She would look out at the sails in the distance and the whole sweep of the estuary from the chateau at Tancarville to the lighthouses at Le Havre. Sometimes the sun would suddenly break through the clouds and make her blink. Afterwards, they

would rest under the arbour. Her mother had procured a little flask of the choicest Malaga wine, from which Virginie would take just two tiny sips, laughing at the thought of making herself tipsy.

She began to recover her strength. Autumn gradually slipped by. Félicité did all she could to reassure Madame Aubain. But one evening, on her way back from an errand in the town, she noticed Monsieur Poupart's gig standing at the front door. Monsieur Poupart himself was in the entrance hall and Madame Aubain was fastening her bonnet.

'Bring me my foot-warmer, my purse and my gloves! Hurry!'

Virginie had pneumonia and Madame feared she was beyond recovery.

'I'm sure it's not that bad,' said the doctor, and the two of them climbed into his carriage, with the snowflakes falling in great flurries around them. Night was drawing on and it was bitterly cold.

Félicité dashed into the church to light a candle and then began to run after Monsieur Poupart's gig. It was a full hour before she caught up with it. She jumped up behind it and clung to the fringe. Suddenly a thought occurred to her. 'The gate to the courtyard was not locked! What if thieves should break in!' She jumped back down on to the road.

The next day, at the very first sign of daylight, she went to the doctor's house. The doctor had returned but had

already left again to visit patients in the country. She waited at the inn, thinking that someone or other might arrive with a letter. Eventually, in the half-light of morning, she boarded the Lisieux stagecoach.

The convent was situated at the foot of a steep narrow street. When she was about half-way down the street, she began to make out strange sounds coming from the convent; it was the tolling of a death bell. 'It must be for someone else', she thought, and gave the door-knocker a loud rap.

After some considerable time, she heard the shuffle of footsteps, the door was inched open and a nun appeared.

The good sister solemnly announced that 'she had just passed away'. At precisely the same moment, the bell of Saint-Léonard's began to toll even more strongly.

Félicité went up to the second floor.

She stood in the doorway of the bedroom and could see Virginie laid out on her back, her hands clasped together, her mouth open and her head tilted backwards. Above her head and inclined towards her was a black crucifix; her face was whiter than the drapes which hung stiffly around her. Madame Aubain lay hugging the foot of the bed and sobbing wildly. The Mother Superior stood beside her on the right. On the chest of drawers, three candlesticks gave out little circles of red light; outside, the fog whitened the window panes. Some nuns came and led Madame Aubain away.

Félicité did not leave Virginie's bedside for two whole

nights. She sat there, repeating the same prayers over and over again; she would get up to sprinkle holy water on the sheets, then come back to her chair and continue to gaze fixedly at the dead girl. At the end of her first night's vigil, she noticed that her face was beginning to turn yellow, her lips were turning blue, her nose had grown thinner and her eyes had become sunken. More than once she kissed her eyes and would not have been in the least surprised if Virginie had opened them again; to minds like hers, the supernatural appears perfectly ordinary. She laid her out, wrapped her in her shroud, put her in her coffin, placed a wreath upon her and spread out her hair. Her hair was fair and amazingly long for a girl of her age. Félicité cut off a large lock of it and slipped half of it into her bosom, resolving that it would never be separated from her.

The body was brought back to Pont-l'Evêque, according to Madame Aubain's instructions. Madame Aubain followed the hearse in a closed carriage.

After the funeral mass, it took another three-quarters of an hour to get to the cemetery. Paul led the procession, sobbing. Monsieur Bourais walked behind him, followed in turn by various dignitaries from Pont-l'Evêque, the women, all wearing black veils, and lastly Félicité. Félicité could not help thinking of her nephew and, having been unable to offer him these last honours, she now felt an added grief, as if he were being buried along with Virginie.

Madame Aubain's despair knew no bounds.

At first she rebelled against God, thinking it was unjust

that He should take her daughter from her when she had never done any wrong and when there was nothing for her to feel guilty about. But perhaps there was. She should have taken her to the South. Other doctors would have cured her. She blamed herself, wished she could follow her daughter to the grave and called out in anguish in the middle of her dreams. One dream in particular tormented her. Her husband, dressed like a sailor, had returned from a long voyage and, choking back his tears, told her that he had received an order to take Virginie away. They then both racked their brains to think of a hiding place for her.

On one occasion she came in from the garden distraught. Just a moment before (and she pointed to the spot), the father and daughter had appeared in front of her, one after the other. They were not doing anything; they were just staring at her.

For several months she remained in her room, totally listless. Félicité gently admonished her, telling her that she should look after herself for the sake of her son and her late husband and in memory of 'her'.

'Her?' said Madame Aubain as though waking from sleep. 'Oh yes, of course. You haven't forgotten her, have you!' This was a reference to the cemetery, which Madame Aubain had been expressly forbidden to visit.

Félicité went there every day.

On the stroke of four, she would walk past the row of houses, climb the hill, open the gate and approach

Virginie's grave. There was a little column of pink marble standing on a stone base, with a small garden surrounded by chains. The separate beds could hardly be seen beneath the covering of flowers. Félicité would water the leaves, place fresh sand on the garden and get down on her hands and knees to make sure the ground was properly weeded. When Madame Aubain was eventually able to come to see the grave, she found it a source of comfort, a kind of consolation for her loss.

The years passed, one very much like another, marked only by the annual recurrence of the church festivals: Easter, the Assumption, All Saints' Day. It was only little incidents in their daily lives that, in later years, enabled them to recall a particular date. Thus in 1825 two glaziers whitewashed the entrance hall; in 1827 a part of the roof fell into the courtyard and nearly killed a passer-by. In the summer of 1828 it was Madame's turn to distribute consecrated bread to the parishioners. This was also about the same time that Bourais mysteriously left the town. One by one, all their old acquaintances went away: Guyot, Liébard, Madame Lechaptois, Robelin and old Uncle Gremanville, who had been paralysed for many years.

One night, the driver of the mail-coach arrived in Pont-l'Evêque with news of the July Revolution. A few days later, a new subprefect was appointed: the Baron de Larsonnière, who had previously been a consul in America. He arrived in Pont-l'Evêque accompanied not only by his wife but also by his sister-in-law and three young

girls, all of them already quite grown up. They were often to be seen on their lawn, dressed in long, flowing smocks. They also had a Negro servant and a parrot. They called on Madame Aubain to pay their respects and she made a point of doing likewise. As soon as she spotted them approaching in the distance, Félicité would come running in to tell Madame Aubain that they were on their way. But there was only one thing that could really awaken her interest and that was her son's letters.

Paul seemed unable to settle down to a career and spent much of his time in the tavern. Madame Aubain would pay off his debts, but he immediately ran up new ones. She would sit at her knitting by the window and heave sighs that Félicité could hear even in the kitchen, where she was working at her spinning wheel.

The two women would often take a stroll together alongside the trellised wall of the garden. They still talked constantly about Virginie, wondering whether she would have liked such and such a thing or trying to imagine what she would have said on such and such an occasion.

All her belongings were still in a cupboard in the children's bedroom. Madame Aubain had avoided looking inside it as much as possible. Then, one summer day, she resigned herself. Moths came flying from the cupboard.

Virginie's frocks hung in a row beneath a shelf upon which there were three dolls, some hoops, a set of doll's furniture and her own hand-basin. The two women took out all the petticoats, stockings and handkerchiefs and

spread them out on the two beds before folding them again. This sorry collection of objects lay there, caught in a beam of sunlight which brought out all the stains and the creases that had been made by the movements of Virginie's body. The air was warm, the sky was blue, a blackbird sang outside and the world seemed to be utterly at peace. They found a little chestnut-coloured hat made of long-piled plush, but it had been completely destroyed by the moths. Félicité asked if she might have it as a keepsake. The two women looked at each other and their eyes filled with tears. Madame Aubain opened her arms and Félicité threw herself into them. Mistress and servant embraced each other, uniting their grief in a kiss which made them equal.

It was the first time that this had ever happened, Madame Aubain being, by nature, very reserved. Félicité could not have been more grateful if she had been offered a priceless gift and from then on she doted on her mistress with dog-like fidelity and the reverence that might be accorded to a saint.

As time went by, Félicité's natural kind-heartedness increased.

One day she heard the sound of drums from a regiment marching along the street and she stood at the door with a jug of cider, handing out drinks to the soldiers. She helped to nurse cholera victims and to look after the refugees from Poland. One of the Poles even said he would like to marry her, but they had a serious argument when she came back one morning from the angelus to find him

ensconced in her kitchen, calmly helping himself to a salad which she had prepared for lunch.

After the Poles had left, she turned her attention to an old man by the name of Colmiche, who was rumoured to have committed terrible atrocities in '93. He now lived down by the river in a ruined pigsty. The boys in the town used to spy on him through the cracks in the wall and throw stones at him as he lay coughing and choking on his straw bed. He had long, straggling hair, his eyelids were inflamed and on one arm there was a swelling bigger than his head. Félicité provided him with linen and did what she could to keep his hovel clean; she even hoped she might be able to install him in the outhouse, where he would not disturb Madame. When the tumour burst, she changed his dressing every single day. Sometimes she would bring him a small piece of cake or help him outside on to a bundle of straw, where he could lie in the sun. The poor old wretch would splutter and shake and thank her in a barely audible whisper, saying he could not bear to lose her and stretching out his hands the minute he saw her preparing to leave him. He died and Félicité had a mass said for the repose of his soul.

On the same day, she received the most wonderful surprise. Just as she was serving dinner, Madame de Larsonnière's Negro servant arrived, carrying the parrot in its cage, along with its perch, chain and padlock. There was a note from the Baroness, informing Madame Aubain that her husband had been promoted to a Préfecture and

that they were leaving Pont-l'Evêque that very evening. She asked Madame Aubain if she would be kind enough to accept the parrot as a memento of their friendship and as a token of her respect.

The parrot had been a source of wonder to Félicité for a long time, for it came from America, a word which always reminded her of Victor. She had already questioned the servant about it and, on one occasion, had even said that 'Madame would be delighted to look after it!'

The Negro had mentioned this to his mistress and, because she could not take it away with her, she readily seized this opportunity of getting it off her hands.

4

The parrot was called Loulou. His body was green, the tips of his wings were pink, the top of his head was blue and his breast was gold-coloured.

Unfortunately, he had the tiresome habit of chewing his perch and he kept plucking out his feathers, scattering his droppings everywhere and splashing the water from his bath all over his cage. He thoroughly irritated Madame Aubain and so she gave him to Félicité to look after.

She decided she would teach him to speak and he was very soon able to say, 'Pretty boy!', 'Your servant, sir!' and 'Hail Mary!' She put him near the front door and a number of visitors were surprised that he would not

answer to the name 'Polly', which is what all parrots are supposed to be called. Some people said he looked more like a turkey or called him a blockhead. Félicité found their jibes very hurtful. There was a curious stubborn streak in Loulou which never ceased to amaze Félicité; he would refuse to talk the minute anyone looked at him!

Even so, there was no doubt that he appreciated company. On Sundays, when the Rochefeuille sisters, Monsieur de Houppeville and some of Madame Aubain's new friends – the apothecary Onfroy, Monsieur Varin and Captain Mathieu – came round to play cards, Loulou would beat on the window panes with his wings and make such a furious commotion that no one could hear themselves speak.

He obviously found Bourais's face a source of great amusement. He only had to see it and he would break into fits of uncontrollable laughter. His squawks could be heard echoing round the yard. The neighbours would come to their windows and start laughing too. To avoid being seen by the parrot, Bourais would slink past the house along the side of the wall, hiding his face behind his hat. He would go down to the river and come into the house by way of the back garden. The looks he gave the bird were not of the tender variety.

The butcher's boy had once flipped Loulou on the ear for trying to help himself to something from his basket and, since then, Loulou always tried to give him a peck through his shirt. Fabu threatened to wring his neck,

although he was not cruel by nature, despite what the tattoos on his arms and his long side whiskers might have led one to believe. In fact, he was rather fond of the parrot and, just for the fun of it, he had even tried to teach him a few swear words. Félicité was alarmed at the thought of his acquiring such bad habits and moved him into the kitchen. His chain was removed and he was allowed to wander all over the house.

When he came down the stairs, he would position the curved part of his beak on the step in front of him and then raise first his right foot, followed by his left. Félicité was always worried that these weird acrobatics would make the parrot giddy. He fell ill and could not talk or eat due to an ulcer under his tongue, such as chickens sometimes have. Félicité cured him herself, extracting the lump in his mouth with her fingernails. One day, Monsieur Paul was silly enough to blow cigar smoke up his nose. On another occasion, when Madame Lormeau was teasing him with the end of her parasol, he bit off the metal ferrule with his beak. Then there was the time he got lost.

Félicité had put him out on the grass to get some fresh air. She went indoors for a minute and, when she came back, the parrot had disappeared. She searched for him in the bushes, by the river and even on the rooftops, oblivious to her mistress's shouts of 'Do be careful! You must be mad!' She then hunted through every single garden in Pont-l'Evêque and stopped all the people in the street, asking, 'You don't happen to have seen my parrot by any

chance?' Those who did not already know the parrot were given a full description. Suddenly, she thought she saw something green flying about behind the mills at the bottom of the hill. But when she got to the top of the hill, there was nothing to be seen. A pedlar told her he had definitely seen the bird only a short while ago in old Madame Simon's shop at Saint-Melaine. Félicité ran all the way there, but nobody knew what she was talking about. In the end she came back home, utterly exhausted, her shoes torn to shreds and feeling sick at heart. She sat down on the middle of the garden bench, next to Madame, and she was telling her everything that she had done when she suddenly felt something drop gently on to her shoulder. It was Loulou! What on earth had he been up to? Perhaps he had just gone for a little walk around the town!

It took Félicité quite a while to recover from this shock. If the truth were known, she never really recovered from it completely.

She caught tonsillitis, as a result of getting thoroughly chilled, and shortly afterwards developed pains in her ears. Within three years she was completely deaf and spoke in a very loud voice, even in church. Even though her sins could have been proclaimed in every corner of the diocese without bringing any discredit to her or causing offence to others, the curé decided that it would now be best to hear her confession in the sacristy.

Imaginary buzzing noises in her head added to her troubles. Her mistress would often say, 'Goodness me!

You're just being silly!' Félicité would answer, 'Yes, Madame,' still looking around her to see where the noises were coming from.

She became enclosed in an ever-diminishing world of her own; gone for ever was the pealing of church bells and the lowing of cattle in the fields. Every living thing passed by her in ghostly silence. Only one sound now reached her ears, and that was the voice of her parrot.

Almost as if he were deliberately trying to entertain her, he would imitate the clicking of the turnspit, the shrill cry of the fishmonger or the sound of sawing from the joiner's shop on the other side of the street. Whenever the front door bell rang, he would imitate Madame Aubain: 'Félicité! The door, the door!'

They would hold conversations with each other, the parrot endlessly repeating the three stock phrases from his repertory and Félicité replying with words that made very little sense but which all came straight from the heart. In her isolation, Loulou was almost a son to her; she simply doted on him. He used to climb up her fingers, peck at her lips and hang on to her shawl. Sometimes she would put her face close to his and shake her head in the way a nurse does to a baby, with the wings of her bonnet and the bird's wings all fluttering together.

When storm clouds gathered and thunder rumbled, the bird would squawk loudly, no doubt remembering the sudden cloud-bursts of his native forests. The sound of falling rain would send him into a frenzy. He would fly

madly about the house, shooting up to the ceiling, knocking everything over and finally escaping through the window into the garden to splash around in the puddles. But he would soon come back, perch on one of the fire-dogs, jump up and down to dry his feathers and then proudly display his tail or his beak.

One morning in the terrible winter of 1837, when she had put him near the fireplace because of the cold, she found him dead in his cage, hanging head downwards with his claws caught in the metal bars. He had probably died of a stroke, but the thought crossed Félicité's mind that he might have been poisoned with parsley and, although there was no definite proof, her suspicions fell on Fabu.

She wept so much that her mistress eventually said, 'Well, why don't you have him stuffed?'

Félicité went to consult the chemist, who had always been kind to the parrot.

He wrote to Le Havre and a man by the name of Fellacher agreed to do the job. But, knowing that the mail-coach sometimes mislaid parcels, Félicité decided that she would take the parrot as far as Honfleur herself.

The road ran between endless lines of apple trees, bare and leafless. Ice lay in the ditches. Dogs barked as she walked past the farms. With her hands tucked under her mantlet and her basket on her arm, Félicité walked briskly along the middle of the road in her little black clogs.

She followed the road through the forest, passed Le Haut-Chêne and eventually reached Saint-Gatien.

On the road behind her, in a cloud of dust and gathering speed on its way down the hill, a mail-coach at full gallop came rushing towards her like a whirlwind. The coachman, seeing that this woman was making no attempt to get out of the way, stood up and looked out over the roof of the carriage and both he and his postilion shouted at her for all their worth. The four horses, which he was vainly trying to rein in, galloped faster and faster towards her and the leading pair struck her as they went by. With a sharp tug on the reins, the coachman forced them to swerve on to the side of the road. In his rage, he raised his arm and lashed out at her with his long whip as the coach lurched past. The blow struck Félicité full across her face and the upper part of her body, and with such force that she fell flat on her back.

The first thing she did when she regained consciousness was to open her basket. Fortunately, Loulou had come to no harm. She felt a burning sensation on her right cheek. She put her hand to her face and saw that her hand was red. She was bleeding.

She sat down on a pile of stones and dabbed her face with her handkerchief. Then she ate a crust of bread which she had brought with her in case she needed it and tried to take her mind off her wound by looking at the parrot.

As she came to the top of the hill at Ecquemauville, she saw the lights of Honfleur twinkling in the night like clusters of stars and, beyond them, the sea, stretching dimly into the distance. She was suddenly overcome with

a fit of giddiness and her wretched childhood, the disappointment of her first love affair, the departure of her nephew and the death of Virginie all came flooding back to her like the waves of an incoming tide, welling up inside her and taking her breath away.

She insisted on speaking personally to the captain of the ship and, although she did not tell him what was in her parcel, she asked him to look after it carefully.

Fellacher kept the parrot for a long time. He kept promising that it would arrive the following week. After six months, he announced that a box had been dispatched, but that was the last they heard of it. Félicité began to fear that Loulou would never come back. 'He has been stolen, I know it!' she thought to herself.

But at last he arrived. And quite magnificent he looked too, perched on a branch which was screwed on to a mahogany plinth, with one foot held raised, his head cocked to one side and holding in his beak a nut which the taxidermist, in order to add a little touch of grandeur, had gilded.

Félicité installed him in her room.

This room, which few were allowed into, was filled with a mixture of religious knick-knacks and other miscellaneous bits and pieces and resembled something between a chapel and a bazaar.

A large wardrobe made it awkward to open the door fully. Opposite the window that looked out on to the garden was a smaller circular window which looked out on to

the courtyard. There was a plain, unsprung bed and beside it a table with a water jug, two combs and a small cake of blue soap on a chipped plate. Fixed to the walls were rosaries, medals, several pictures of the Virgin and a holy-water stoop made out of a coconut shell. On the chest of drawers, which was draped with a cloth like an altar, was the shell box that Victor had given her, a watering can and a ball, some handwriting books, the illustrated geography book and a pair of little ankle boots. Hanging by its two ribbons from the nail which supported the mirror was the little plush hat! These keepsakes meant so much to Félicité. She had even kept one of Monsieur's frock-coats. If there was anything that Madame Aubain wanted to get rid of, she would find a place for it in her room, like the artificial flowers beside her chest of drawers and the portrait of the Comte d'Artois in the window recess.

Loulou was placed on a little shelf made especially for the purpose and fixed to a chimney breast which protruded into the room. Every morning, as she woke, she would catch sight of him in the early morning light and would recall the days gone by, trivial incidents, right down to the tiniest detail, remembered not in sadness but in perfect tranquillity.

Being unable to hold a conversation with anyone, she lived her life as if in a sleepwalker's trance. The only thing that seemed capable of bringing her back to life was the Corpus Christi procession, when she would visit all the neighbours, collecting candlesticks and mats to

decorate the altar of repose that was always set up outside in the street.

When she went to church, she would sit gazing at the picture of the Holy Spirit and it struck her that it looked rather like her parrot. The resemblance was even more striking in an Epinal colour print depicting Our Lord's baptism. The dove had wings of crimson and a body of emerald-green and it looked for all the world like Loulou. Félicité bought the picture and hung it in place of the portrait of the Comte d'Artois, so that she could see them both together at the same time. In her mind, the one became associated with the other, the parrot becoming sanctified by connection with the Holy Spirit and the Holy Spirit in turn acquiring added life and meaning. Surely it could not have been a dove that God had chosen to speak through, since doves cannot talk. It must have been one of Loulou's ancestors. Félicité would say her prayers with her eyes turned towards the picture but every now and then she would turn her head slightly to look at the parrot.

She thought of entering the sisterhood of the Ladies of the Virgin but Madame Aubain persuaded her not to.

There now occurred an event of considerable importance – Paul's wedding.

Having worked first as a lawyer's clerk, Paul had subsequently tried his hand at business, worked for the Customs and for the Inland Revenue and had even considered joining the Department of Forests and Waterways. Now, at the age of thirty-six, as if by divine inspiration,

he had suddenly discovered his vocation – the Registry Office! Indeed, he had displayed such a talent for the job that one of the inspectors had offered him his daughter's hand in marriage and had promised to use his influence to advance his career.

By now, Paul took his responsibilities seriously and he brought his intended to see his mother.

Not a thing at Pont-l'Evêque met with her approval. She expected to be treated like royalty and she hurt Félicité's feelings badly. Madame Aubain was relieved to see her go.

The following week, they learned of the death of Monsieur Bourais in an inn somewhere in Lower Brittany. Rumour had it that he had committed suicide. This turned out to be true and questions were raised about his honesty. Madame Aubain went through her accounts and the catalogue of his misdeeds soon became apparent: embezzlement of arrears of rent, undeclared sales of wood, forged receipts, and so forth. It was also discovered that he was the father of an illegitimate child and that he was having 'an illicit relationship with someone from Dozulé'.

This sordid business was a source of great distress to Madame Aubain. In March 1853, she began to feel pains in her chest. A grey coating covered her tongue. She was treated with leeches but this failed to improve her breathing. On the ninth evening of her illness, she died, aged just seventy-two.

People took her to be younger than this because of her dark hair, which she had always worn in bandeaux round

her pale, pockmarked face. She had very few friends to lament her death; there was a certain haughtiness about her that had always kept people at a distance.

Félicité wept for her in a way that servants rarely weep for their masters. That Madame should die before her disturbed her whole way of thinking; it seemed to go against the natural order of things; it was something unacceptable and unreal.

Ten days later, just as soon as they could get there from Besançon, the heirs arrived on the scene. Madame Aubain's daughter-in-law went through all the drawers, chose a few pieces of furniture for herself and sold what was left. Then they all went back to the Registry Office.

Madame's armchair, her little table, her foot-warmer and the eight chairs had all gone! On the walls, yellow patches marked the places where pictures had once hung. They had taken away the children's beds, along with their mattresses, and the cupboard had been cleared of all Virginie's things. Félicité went from room to room, heartbroken.

The following day, a notice appeared on the front door. The apothecary shouted into Félicité's ear that the house was for sale.

Félicité's head began to swim and she had to sit down.

What most upset her was the thought of having to move out of her own room; it was the perfect place for poor Loulou. In her anguish she would gaze at him and beg the Holy Spirit to come to her aid. She developed the

idolatrous habit of kneeling in front of the parrot to say her prayers. Sometimes the sun would catch the parrot's glass eye as it came through the little window, causing an emanation of radiant light that sent her into ecstasies.

Félicité had been left a pension of three hundred and eighty francs by her mistress. The garden provided her with vegetables. As for clothes, she had sufficient to last her her lifetime and she saved on lighting by going to bed as soon as it began to get dark.

She hardly ever went out, because she disliked walking past the secondhand dealer's shop, where some of the old furniture was on display. Ever since her fit of giddiness, she had been dragging one leg and, as she was now growing frail, old Madame Simon, whose grocery business had recently collapsed, used to come round every morning to chop her firewood and draw her water.

Her eyes grew weaker. The shutters were no longer opened. Many years passed. Nobody came to rent the house and nobody came to buy it.

Félicité never asked for any repairs to be done, because she was frightened she might be evicted. The laths in the roof rotted and for one whole winter her bolster was permanently wet from the rain. Shortly after Easter, she coughed blood.

Madame Simon called for a doctor. Félicité wanted to know what was wrong with her. But by now she was too deaf to hear what was said and she only managed to catch one word: 'pneumonia'. It was a word she knew and she

quietly answered, 'Ah! Like Madame', finding it quite natural that she should follow in her mistress's footsteps.

The time for preparing the altars of repose was drawing near.

The first of them was always placed at the foot of the hill, the second outside the post office and the third about half-way up the street. The exact position of this last altar was a matter of some rivalry, but the women of the parish eventually agreed that it should be placed in Madame Aubain's courtyard.

Félicité's breathing was getting worse and she was becoming more feverish. She fretted at not being able to do anything for the altar. If only there were at least something that she could put on it! And then she thought of the parrot. The neighbours objected, saying that it was not really suitable. But the curé gave his permission and this made Félicité so happy that she asked him to accept Loulou, the one treasure she possessed, as a gift from her when she died.

From Tuesday to Saturday, the eve of Corpus Christi, her coughing increased. By the evening, her face looked drawn, her lips were sticking to her gums and she began vomiting. The following morning, at first light, feeling very low, she sent for a priest. Three good women stood round her as she was given extreme unction. She then announced that she needed to speak to Fabu.

Fabu arrived dressed in his Sunday best and feeling very ill at ease in such sombre surroundings.

'Please forgive me,' she said, summoning all her

strength to extend her arm towards him, 'I thought it was you who had killed him.'

What was all this nonsense? How could she suspect someone like him of having committed a murder! Fabu was most indignant and was on the point of losing his temper.

'Her mind is wandering,' they said. 'Surely you can see that.'

From time to time Félicité seemed to be speaking to phantoms. The women went away. Madame Simon ate her lunch.

A little later she went to fetch Loulou and held him close to Félicité. 'Come on,' she said. 'Say goodbye to him.'

Although Loulou was not a corpse, he was being eaten away by maggots. One of his wings was broken and the stuffing was coming out of his stomach. But Félicité was now blind. She kissed him on his forehead and held him against her cheek. Madame Simon took him from her and went to replace him on the altar.

5

The smells of summer drifted in from the meadows. The air was filled with the buzzing of flies. The sun glinted on the surface of the river and warmed the slates of the roof. Madame Simon had come back into the room and was gently nodding off to sleep.

She was awoken by the sound of bells; they were coming out of vespers. Félicité grew suddenly calmer. She thought of the procession and saw everything as clearly as if she were there.

All the schoolchildren, the choristers and the firemen were walking along the pavements. In the middle of the street, at the head of the procession, came the church officer with his halberd, the beadle carrying the great cross, the schoolmaster in charge of the boys and the nun keeping a motherly eye on the girls. Three of the prettiest, looking like curly headed angels, were throwing rose petals in the air. They were followed by the deacon conducting the band with arms outstretched and two censer-bearers turning round at every step to face the Holy Sacrament, which was carried by Monsieur le Curé, clad in his magnificent chasuble and protected by a canopy of bright red velvet held aloft by four churchwardens. A great throng of people followed on behind as the procession made its way between the white sheets which draped the walls of the houses and eventually arrived at the bottom of the hill.

Félicité's forehead was bathed in a cold sweat. Madame Simon sponged it with a cloth, telling herself that one day she would go the same way.

The noise of the crowd gradually increased, at one point becoming very loud and then fading away.

A sudden burst of gunfire rattled the window panes. The postilions were saluting the monstrance. Félicité

rolled her eyes and, trying to raise her voice above a whisper, she asked, 'Is he all right?' She was still worrying about the parrot.

Félicité was now entering her final moments. Her breath came in short raucous gasps, making her sides heave. Beads of froth gathered in the corners of her mouth and her whole body began to shake.

From the street outside came the blaring of ophicleides, the high-pitched voices of the children and the deeper voices of the men. There were moments when all was quiet and all that could be heard was the tread of feet, cushioned by the scattered petals and sounding like a flock of sheep crossing a field.

The group of clergy entered the courtyard. Madame Simon climbed up on to a chair to look out of the little window and was able to see the altar directly below.

It was hung with green garlands and covered with a flounce in English point lace. Standing in the centre was a little square frame containing some relics and at each end there was an orange tree. Along the length of the altar there was a row of silver candlesticks and china vases containing a vivid display of sunflowers, lilies, peonies, foxgloves and bunches of hydrangea. A cascade of bright colours fell from the top of the altar down to the carpet spread out on the cobblestones beneath it. In amongst the flowers could be seen a number of other treasured ornaments: a silver-gilt sugar-bowl decorated with a ring of violets, a set of pendants cut from Alençon gemstones

glittering on a little carpet of moss, two Chinese screens with painted landscapes. Loulou lay hidden beneath some roses and all that could be seen of him was the spot of blue on the top of his head, like a disc of lapis lazuli.

The churchwardens, the choristers and the children took up their places around three sides of the courtyard. The priest slowly walked up the steps and placed his great shining orb on the lace altar cloth. Everyone fell to their knees. There was a deep silence in which all that could be heard was the sound of the censers sliding on their chains as they were swung backwards and forwards.

A blue haze of incense floated up into Félicité's room. She opened her nostrils wide to breathe it in, savouring it with mystical fervour. Her eyes closed and a smile played on her lips. One by one her heartbeats became slower, growing successively weaker and fainter like a fountain running dry, an echo fading away. With her dying breath she imagined she saw a huge parrot hovering above her head as the heavens parted to receive her.

PENGUIN

LITTLE BLACK

CLASSICS

PENGUIN

LITTLE BLACK

CLASSICS

“她决心教他说话，
而且没过多久，
他便会说：
‘好孩子！’
‘您的仆人，先生！’
‘万福玛利亚！’”

PENGUIN

LITTLE BLACK

CLASSICS

一颗简单的心

A Simple Heart

［法］福楼拜 著

余西 译

中信出版集团 · 北京

图书在版编目（CIP）数据

企鹅经典 · 小黑书 . 第一辑 : 英、汉 / (日) 吉田兼好等著 ; 文东等译 . -- 北京 : 中信出版社 , 2018.11(2022.7 重印)

书名原文 : Penguin Little Black Classics

ISBN 978-7-5086-9400-9

Ⅰ . ①企… Ⅱ . ①吉… ②文… Ⅲ . ①世界文学－作品综合集－英、汉 Ⅳ . ① I11

中国版本图书馆 CIP 数据核字 (2018) 第 193780 号

A Simple Heart

企鹅经典：小黑书　第一辑

一颗简单的心

著　　者：[法] 福楼拜
译　　者：余 西
出版发行：中信出版集团股份有限公司
（北京市朝阳区惠新东街甲 4 号富盛大厦 2 座 邮编 100029）
承 印 者：河北鹏润印刷有限公司

开　　本：787mm×1092mm　1/32　　印　　张：41　　字　　数：300 千字
版　　次：2018 年 11 月第 1 版　　印　　次：2022 年 7 月第13次印刷
京权图字：01-2018-6477
书　　号：ISBN 978-7-5086-9400-9
定　　价：149.00 元（全 10 册）

服务热线：400-600-8099
投稿邮箱：author@citicpub.com

一

欧班夫人的女仆费莉西泰，让蓬莱韦克那些好太太羡慕了整整半个世纪。

她一年的工钱也就一百法郎，却包揽了所有下厨房的事和家务活。她缝补，清洗，熨烫衣裳；套马，喂养家禽，炼制奶油。不仅如此，她对女主人也一直忠心耿耿，而我们得说，那女主人可不好相处。

欧班夫人嫁给了一位英俊而贫穷的年轻人。一八〇九年初，他过世了，留下她和两个年幼的孩子，以及一笔数额可观的债务。她只好变卖家产，仅留下图克和热福塞两处的农庄。这两处农庄一年能提供给她的租金收入，最多不过五千法郎。为了维持生计，她只好搬出圣梅兰的住宅，住进一栋相对便宜的房子。那房子本是她家族

的，坐落在集市后面。

这栋房子有着石板瓦屋顶，在一条小巷和一条通往河边的窄街之间。房子里，地面高低不平，走在上面很容易被绊倒。一条狭窄的过道隔开了厨房与起居室。欧班夫人整日待在起居室，坐在平开窗前一张柳条编的扶手椅上。一排八张红木椅靠着白漆护壁板。晴雨表挂在墙上，下方是架古旧的钢琴。各种小包裹、纸板箱在钢琴上堆得高高的，像一座金字塔。两张铺着挂毯的简易椅，分别放置在路易十五风格的黄色大理石壁炉旁。一只钟，挂在壁炉上方的中央，设计得像座维斯塔神庙。整个房间散发着霉味，那是因为地面比花园低的缘故。

二楼，有一间“夫人”的卧室。那是一个很大的房间，装饰着暗淡的、带有花纹的墙纸。墙上挂着幅“老爷”的画像，他穿着在那时很时髦的奇特服装。卧室径直通往一个更小的房间，里面放着两张孩子的床，每张床的垫子都被移走了。再过去便是客厅，常年关闭，堆满了蒙着布罩的家具。最后，有一个过道通向书房。堆着书和纸的书橱，占据了三面墙，将一个很大的乌木书桌包围其中。书橱的侧板上贴满了素描画、水粉风景画，

以及奥德朗的版画，让人想起已然逝去的美好时日，以及更奢华的品位。三楼是费莉西泰的卧室，被天窗所照亮。窗外，可以见到牧场。

费莉西泰总在天蒙蒙亮时起床，以确保能赶上弥撒。之后，她便一口气也不歇地劳作到晚上。晚餐结束后，她收拾好陶盘，紧实地闩上门，用灰烬埋了柴火，便手拿念珠，在壁炉前睡去了。在讨价还价时，没人能比她更固执。而论干净，她洗刷的平底小圆锅，足以让蓬莱韦克别家的女仆绝望。她从不浪费，吃得很慢，还会用手指把掉在桌上的面包屑沾干净。那面包是专为她烤的，足有十二磅，能让她吃上二十天。

无论遇上什么天气，她都披一条印花方头巾，用别针扣在后面，戴一顶完全盖住头发的女帽，穿一双灰色长筒袜、一条红色裙子，再在上衣外面罩着背带围裙，像医院护士穿的那样。

她的脸是瘦削的，声音是尖锐的。二十五岁时，人们以为她有四十岁。而在她五十岁生日过后，倒让人越发难以看出她的年纪了。她不怎么说话，身板挺直，步调僵硬，就像一位被发条驱使的、木头做的女人。

二

和别的女孩一样，她也曾恋爱过。

她的父亲是个石匠，从脚手架上跌下来摔死了。随后，母亲过世，姐姐们也各自谋生去了。一个农民收留了她。尽管她还很小，仍被派去牧场看顾牛群。她总是衣不遮体，冷得直哆嗦；趴在地上喝池塘里的水。她经常毫无缘由地挨打，最后被赶出了房子，说是她偷了三十苏[1]，但她其实是无辜的。后来，她在别的农场找了份工作，饲养家禽。雇主喜爱她，却招来了朋友们的妒忌。

八月的一个晚上（那时她十八岁），她被拉去参加科勒维尔的乡村游园会。喧闹的提琴声、树上的彩灯、一件件绚丽多彩的衣裳、金色的十字架和丝带，以及那些随音乐跳动的人，一时间让她茫然不知所措。她独自站在一旁，怯生生的。一个看起来很有钱的年轻人，靠在农场马车的车轴上抽着烟斗。他走来，邀请她跳舞。他为她买了一杯苹果汁、一杯咖啡、一个蛋糕和一条丝绸围巾。他想着她已领会了他的意思，便提议送她回家。走到燕麦田边时，他将她推倒在地。她害怕地尖叫起来。

1. 苏（sou），法国曾发行的一种铜币。——译者注

他跑了。

不久后的一个晚上，她在前往博蒙特的路上遇到一辆大车。车子载着干草，缓慢笨拙地前行着。她想超过它。在挨着车轮走过去的时候，她认出车上的人是泰奥多尔。

他面无愧色地看着她，说她理应原谅他那晚的行为，毕竟他“那晚只是喝多了”。

她不知该如何作答，只想逃走。

于是，他转换话题，谈起了当年的收成，以及这个地区的各大人物。他说，他父亲已离开科勒维尔，在艾科特买了处农庄，也就是说，他们现在是邻居了。她回应说:“哦，这样啊！”他说，他父母希望他安定下来，但他不着急，更愿意在结婚前遇见那个对的女人。她听了，垂下双眼。他问，她是否正考虑结婚的事情。她笑了，说他那样取笑她可不好。“但我发誓，我不是在取笑你。”他说着，伸出左手，搂住了她的腰。她就这样让他搂着，继续往前走。现在，他们走得更慢了。微风徐徐，星辰闪耀。在他们面前，大马车上的干草来回晃动。四匹马艰难地踱步向前，起了片片尘土。未经任何指令，马儿向右转了。这时，他吻了吻她，而她在夜色里逃开了。

接下来的那周，泰奥多尔约她出来了几次。

他们在农家院子的角落里碰面，躲在墙后或一棵树下。费莉西泰并不像同龄的年轻姑娘那般懵懂无知。和农场牲口打交道，让她学会了很多。然而，她与生俱来的慎重，以及保持贞洁的本能，使她避免了屈从泰奥多尔的欲求。她这般推阻，让泰奥多尔很是泄气。为了满足欲望（或者，也可能是出于单纯的想法），他开始向她求婚。她不知道是否该相信他，而他则坚持说自己是认真的。

不久，他说起一件烦心的事：一年前，他父母花钱让人代他服兵役，但他仍有可能随时被征召。一想起有这种可能，他就害怕。费莉西泰将这种怯懦看成是爱的讯息，这让她更爱他了。夜里，她从房子里溜出来去见泰奥多尔，而他则用忧惧和哀求，向她发起进攻。

最终，他说他要亲自去市政府查探情况。他会在下个星期天的十一点至午夜间回来，告诉费莉西泰结果。

到了约定的时间，费莉西泰去见她的情人。

但她见到的并不是泰奥多尔，而是他的一个朋友。

他告诉她，她再也不会见到泰奥多尔了。为了确保不被征召入伍，他娶了图克一个有钱的老女人，勒胡塞

太太。

费莉西泰很悲伤。她扑倒在地，号啕痛哭；她祈求上天的帮助，独自一人躺在田野里，哭到天亮。然后，她回到农场，说她决定要离开了。到了月底，她领了工钱，将几样东西用披巾包好，便前往蓬莱韦克了。

她来到一家客栈前，向一个戴寡妇帽的女人打听。正好她也在找一个厨子。这位年轻的姑娘对烹饪所知不多，但似乎很乐意学习，而且随时准备帮忙，于是欧班夫人最后说："那好吧，就你了。"

一刻钟后，费莉西泰就在她家安置下来。

起初，她时常感到不安，因为这家人规矩很多，而对"老爷"的怀念似乎徘徊在所有事物之上。维尔吉妮和保罗，一个七岁，一个只有四岁，都像是某种珍贵的材料做的。她喜欢像马似的驮着他们，只在欧班夫人不许她老是亲吻他们时，才会让她觉得受了委屈。即使如此，她仍很快乐。新的环境很舒适，她早先的不愉快很快就消散了。

每逢周四，欧班夫人的朋友会来玩波士顿牌。费莉西泰事先备好了纸牌和暖脚炉。客人们总是八点准时到，十一点钟声响起时离开。

每周一早上，在小巷尽头有家店面的旧货商，会在人行道上摆出各种零碎的五金器件。整个城镇充满了嘈杂的声响，有马嘶、羊叫、猪哼，以及马车驶过街面的咔嗒声。正午左右，也就是集市最繁忙的时候，一个老农会跨上台阶，前来拜访欧班夫人。他身材高大，鹰钩鼻，脑后面歪戴着顶帽子。他叫罗伯兰，来自热福塞农场。随之而来的，是图克农场的里埃巴。他又矮又胖，脸色红润，穿着一件灰夹克，长筒皮靴上绑着马刺。

他们俩都带着鸡或奶酪，想着办法让女地主能买下来。但无论要什么把戏，费莉西泰总能赢过他们，他们也因此总是很尊敬她。

有时，欧班夫人也会接待她的叔叔，德·格莱芒维特侯爵。他因生活放纵，败光了所有的钱财。现在，住在法莱斯仅剩的一小块领地上。他总是在午餐时间来，带着一条惹人厌的小贵宾犬，它会在家具上涂满泥爪印。他表现得像一位绅士，每次提及“先父”，总会抬一下帽子。但终究恶习难改，很快他就会给自己倒上一杯又一杯酒，尽说一些下流的玩笑话。费莉西泰会礼貌地将他带到门边，说：“我想，今天差不多了，德·格莱芒维特侯爵！下回再来看我们吧！”说完，便把他关在了门外。

不过，她倒是很乐意迎接退休的律师布雷先生。他的白领带、秃脑门、衬衫前襟上的荷叶花边、宽大的棕色大衣、捏鼻烟时弯起胳膊的独特姿态——事实上，有关这个人的一切，都让费莉西泰心慌意乱，就像我们见到大人物时那样。

他替“夫人”照管产业，会连着好几小时和夫人关在“老爷”的书房里。他总担心名誉受损，对法院尊敬万分，并声称自己懂一些拉丁文。

他给孩子们买了一本带插图的地理书，因为他认为这将有利于他们从学习中得到乐趣。这本书描述了世界各地的场景：戴着羽毛头饰的食人族，一只诱拐年轻女孩的猴子，一群沙漠中的贝都因人，一条中了鱼叉的鲸鱼，等等。

保罗将所有这些插图仔细地讲解给费莉西泰听。实际上，这是唯一一次有人教她如何阅读一本书。

给孩子们上课的是居尤，那是一个着实可怜的家伙。他在镇公所工作，因写一手好字而出名，喜欢在靴底磨砺他的笔刀。

一旦天气晴好，全家都会起得早早的，前往热福塞农庄消磨一整天。

院子坐落在斜坡上，农舍则在院子中央。从那里可以望见远处的海，像一条小小的灰色带子。

费莉西泰从篮子里拿出片片冷肉。他们在挨着牛奶房的房间里吃饭。那个房间是已然塌毁的乡村别墅中唯一残存的部分。墙纸剥落，垂了下来，随穿堂风摆动着。欧班夫人低着头，沉浸在往事里。这让孩子们几乎不敢说话。她说："你们去玩吧。"于是，他们就走开了。

保罗会爬上谷仓，捉小鸟，在池塘里打水漂，或用木杖敲打大木桶，发出轰隆轰隆的响声，像在敲鼓。

维尔吉妮会去喂兔子，或跑过牧场去采矢车菊。她跑的时候，会露出靓丽的绣花短裤。

秋天的一个晚上，他们穿过草地回家。

上弦月照亮了天空。薄雾飘移着，像纱一样蒙在图克河蜿蜒的水面上。有一群牛躺在草地中央，慵懒地看着他们路过。到了第三块草地，一些牛站起来，在他们面前围成一个圈。费莉西泰说："不用怕！"她边往前走，边哼着引人沉思的小调。来到最近的动物旁，她轻轻拍着它的背脊。它走开了，其他的牛也一样。然而，刚穿过下块草地，他们就听到一声可怕的牛哞。那是一头隐藏在雾中的公牛。它开始朝那两位女士走来。欧班夫人

想逃走。费莉西泰说:“不不，不能走得太快！”但她们却走得更快了。即使如此，她们仍能听到身后越来越近的公牛鼻息，以及牛蹄捶打青草的声响。她们知道它正飞奔而来。费莉西泰转身，面对公牛，从地上捡起土块，扔向它的脸。公牛低下头，晃着双角，颤抖着发出怒吼。现在，欧班夫人带着两个孩子，已到了草地边，急着想穿过树篱。费莉西泰则面对公牛，仍有条不紊地撤退，将一块草根土扔进它的眼睛里，一边还喊着:“快，快！”

欧班夫人下了沟底，相继推着维尔吉妮和保罗上去了。她爬堤岸时，跌落了几次。不过最终还是凭着股子意志力，成功地爬了上去。

公牛已将费莉西泰逼到一扇栅栏门前，喷吐的口水溅到了她脸上。下一秒，牛角就要顶到她了。在这危急时刻，她竟从两根木桩之间硬挤了过去。这庞大的家伙吓了一跳，愣在了原地。

多年以后，蓬莱韦克的人仍会谈起这桩历险。但费莉西泰并不引以为傲，也丝毫不觉得她的作为有什么英勇可言。

维尔吉妮占据了她全部的心神。那场公牛带来的可怕经历，已影响了维尔吉妮的神经。普帕特医生建议她

到特鲁维尔洗海水浴。

那时候，还鲜有人来这处风景胜地。欧班夫人四处打听，还请教了布雷先生，做了充分准备，仿佛是一场很漫长的旅程。

临行前一天，行李由里埃巴的农场马车送走了。第二天，他牵着两匹马回来。一匹有女士马鞍，带着天鹅绒靠背。另一匹马的背上放着一个斗篷卷成的坐垫。欧班夫人骑上马，跟在里埃巴后头。费莉西泰在另一匹马上照顾维尔吉妮。保罗骑的则是夏勒杜瓦先生的驴。借这头驴，有一个明确的条件，他们得精心照顾它。

路况很糟。五英里的路，他们走了两小时。马匹踩在泥地里，陷到踝骨。它们得猛然向前，才能自如地拔出脚来。它们的脚绊在车辙里，有时不得不跳一下。在路上的某些地方，里埃巴的母马突然不走了。里埃巴耐心等着，直到它再次走动。骑行时，他会说起住在路旁那些人的故事，并总是额外添加些许个人的评判。比如，到了图克镇中心，他们行经一栋房子，窗外围着簇旱金莲。他耸耸肩，说："这里住着一位勒胡塞太太，她倒不挑年轻人，反而……"费莉西泰没有听到下文，因为这时马儿开始慢跑起来，驴也在前头跑了。他们下了条小

道，一扇门开了，出来两位年轻的农场工人。他们就在农舍门外的肥料堆旁下了马。

里埃巴老夫人迎接女东家，一脸的欢喜溢于言表。午饭时，她摆出牛里脊、大肠、灌肠、奶油炖鸡块、泛着泡沫的果汁、水果馅饼、酒浸李子。全程都在说着恭维的话，说夫人看起来“气色更好了”，说小姐已长成一位“美丽的少女”，说少爷保罗是个多“壮实”的年轻人，还不忘提及他们过世的祖父母。里埃巴一家数代为他们服务，因此老一辈的人也都认识。这农场和里埃巴一家一样，透着股陈旧年代的味道。虫子蛀蚀了房顶的横梁，烟熏黑了墙面，尘土蒙上了窗玻璃。一个橡木架上堆着各种工具：水壶、碟子、锡盘、捕狼器、剪羊毛的大剪刀，以及一个让孩子们觉得格外逗乐的巨大的灌肠器。外面有三所院子，那里的每棵树都长着蘑菇，许多树枝中间生着槲寄生。有些树被风吹倒了，但在树干绽裂的地方又重新长出来。在果实的重压下，所有的树都弯了。茅草屋顶像是厚薄不一的棕色天鹅绒，倒是经受住了最猛烈的风，但马车房坍塌了。欧班夫人说，她会安排人去修的，接着就让人备马去了。

他们花了半小时，来到特鲁维尔。这支小小的旅行

队伍，在来到文考尔——一座从船上方延展的悬崖时，不得不下了马。三分钟后，他们来到码头的一端，进了大卫老夫人的客栈“金色羊羔”的院子。

由于空气变换，以及海水浴的关系，维尔吉妮很快就康复了。她没有泳衣，是穿着衬衫下水的。她的女仆会在一间海关人员的简陋小屋帮她穿衣服，这间小屋也供淋浴的人使用。

下午，他们骑驴走过罗切斯-诺雷斯，去往恩克维尔。起初，小道在像公园草地般轻柔起伏的牧场间蜿蜒攀升。接着，便来到一片高原，那里是牧场和耕地。小道旁种植着冬青，与杂乱的树莓丛长在一起。一棵枯死的大树，其枝丫呈之字形，横亘在蓝天下。

他们总是在一块特定的草地停下休息。往下看，左边是多维尔，右边是勒阿弗尔。前方则是开阔的海。在阳光下，大海散发着微光，像镜面一样光滑。四周围很安静，几乎能听到海浪持续而低沉的声音。麻雀在附近吱吱叫着。巨大的天穹铺展在上方。欧班夫人坐在那里，做着针线活儿。维尔吉妮坐在她身旁，编织着灯芯草。费莉西泰采摘一束束野生薰衣草。而保罗则很无聊，总想着早点上路。

别的时候，他们坐船渡过图克河，去找贝壳。退潮时，海胆、鲍鱼、水母被留在沙滩上。孩子们追逐风吹来的星星点点的泡沫。波浪从海滩一边到另一边，慵懒地破碎在沙子里。海滩延展着，没有边际，但在陆地那一侧，以沙丘为界，将它和跑马场似的玛黑大牧场分隔开来。他们穿过牧场，往回走向特鲁维尔——它就躺在山脚下，每走一步，这座小镇就大一些。各式房子错落开来，像花园里缤纷的花朵。

天气热的时候，他们便待在房间里。外面炫目的光透过百叶窗的缝隙，投进一道道光束。乡村里听不到一丝声响。没有一个人敢冒险来到大街上。占据一切的寂静，让万物显得更为平静。远处，传来船工的锤子在敲打船体的声音，而柏油的气息也随着倦怠的微风飘荡而来。

一天中最激动人心的事，发生在渔船归来的时候。一旦过了入口浮标，他们便开始迂回前进。他们的主帆降到桅杆的一半高，前帆膨胀，像巨大的气球。他们滑过飞溅的海浪，直达海港的中央，随后便突然抛锚。渔船被带到码头后，水手吊起他们的鱼，扔到岸上。鱼还是活的，轻微颤动着。一排马车早就等在那里了。戴着

棉布帽的女人们冲向前，去拿篮子，亲吻她们的男人。

有一天，有个女人向费莉西泰走来。不久，费莉西泰便兴冲冲地回到客栈的房间。她找到了失散姐妹中的一个，这位纳斯塔西·巴奈特，也就是勒鲁夫人，紧随其后进了房间，怀里抱着一个宝宝。一个小孩握着她的右手，而她的左手边是一个小水手。他的手放在臀部上，贝雷帽扣到了耳朵上。

一刻钟后，欧班太太就让她走了。

但之后并没有摆脱他们。他们会刚好等在厨房外面，或者在她们外出散步时，尾随而来。至于那个丈夫，则一直没有现身。

费莉西泰倒是很依恋他们。她给他们买了一条毯子、几件衬衫，和一只炉子。他们很明显在利用她。欧班夫人对费莉西泰这种软心肠很是懊恼。她也反对那个外甥对保罗所表现出的亲密举止。再加上，维尔吉妮犯了咳嗽，天气也更恶劣了，她便返回了蓬莱韦克。

在为保罗选择一所好学校时，布雷先生提了建议。在康城有所公认是最好的学校。因此保罗就被送到了康城。他告别时很勇敢，为即将住在一个会有自己朋友的地方而心满意足。

欧班夫人只好任由她儿子离去，因为她知道他必将获得良好的教育。维尔吉妮很快就适应了，倒是费莉西泰发现，没有他，房子变得太安静了。不过，很快地就有别的事吸引了她的注意力。圣诞节后，她每天得带着维尔吉妮去学习教理问答。

三

费莉西泰进门时，屈膝行了个礼，沿着教堂中堂高耸的天花板下方的过道一路走来，打开欧班夫人坐的教堂长椅的挡门后，自行坐下，环顾了一下四周。

孩子们已在唱诗班的席位入座，男孩在右，女孩居左。神父站在他们前面，靠近读经台。在后殿，一扇彩色玻璃上显示着圣灵在俯视圣母玛利亚。另一扇窗上，则是圣母跪在圣婴耶稣前面。神龛的背后是圣米迦勒屠龙的木雕。

神父开始讲起圣典的梗概。于是，费莉西泰的脑子里便满是伊甸园、大洪水、巴别塔、大火焚毁的城市、灭亡的种族，以及被推倒的偶像。这绚烂的叙事慢慢灌输给她，让她充满了对天父的尊崇，以及对天谴的极度

恐惧。听到耶稣受难的故事，她哭了。他们为什么要将他钉在十字架上？既然他对孩子那么善良，他给饥饿的人以粮食，让盲人重见光明；既然他已被选中，出于温和的天性，选择降生于穷人家一座马厩的麦秆堆上。播种与收获，葡萄树上的果实，所有这些在福音书里提及的常见事物，也在她的生活里头出现。现在，有了与上帝的联系，这些事物更显神圣了。费莉西泰比以往更爱羊羔，因为她爱上帝的羔羊。而鸽子则会让她想起圣灵。

她发现很难想象圣灵到底是什么模样，因为他不仅是一只鸟，有时还是火，有时则是气息。入夜时，她看到在沼泽闪耀的，可能就是圣灵的光；或者是他的气息促使云朵飘过天空；或者是他的声音让教堂的钟声如此悦耳动听。她坐在那里，沉浸于对这些奇迹的敬仰之中，在石头墙的冰凉和教堂的平和里感到身心愉悦。

她丝毫也不理解教义，也没有想过去理解。当神父站着给孩子们讲解，而孩子们重复着所学的时候，费莉西泰睡着了，直到孩子们离开教堂，木屐拍打着石头地面所发出的声响才将她惊醒。就这样，费莉西泰靠着听孩子们背诵，学到了她的教理问答，而这种宗教教育在她年轻时却被忽略了。此后，她便模仿起维尔吉妮的宗

教戒律。她斋戒，她也斋戒。无论她何时去忏悔，她便跟着去。为了圣体瞻礼节，费莉西泰和维尔吉妮还一起做了个圣坛。

维尔吉妮初次领圣餐的前几天，费莉西泰为要准备什么而着急。她担忧她的鞋子，她的念珠，她的弥撒用书，她的手套。她帮着欧班夫人给维尔吉妮穿衣服的时候，手一直在抖。

整个弥撒期间，她都焦虑不安。唱诗班的一侧被布雷先生挡住了，她看不见。但在正对面，她能看见一群女孩，低垂着面纱，戴着白色花冠，看上去像是一片雪地。即使隔着一段距离，她仍能从那线条优美的脖颈、虔诚沉思的情态，认出她深爱的小维尔吉妮。钟声响了。他们全都在静默中低下头，跪了下来。接着，伴随着管风琴强而有力的演奏，唱诗班和教众唱起了《上帝的羔羊》。男孩们列队向前，女孩们随之站起身来。她们双手合十，祈祷着，缓慢地走向点着蜡烛的圣坛。她们一个接一个地跪在圣坛台阶上，领受圣餐，又以相同的顺序，返回到唱诗班的位置。轮到维尔吉妮时，费莉西泰倾身向前，以便能看到她。带着那种出于真爱的非凡想象，她觉得自己就是维尔吉妮本人，借用了她的表情，穿着

她的衣服，用她的心在她的胸口跳动。维尔吉妮张开嘴时，费莉西泰闭上眼睛，几乎要晕厥过去。

第二天一早，费莉西泰前往圣器室，请求给予她圣餐。她带着应有的钦敬领受圣餐，但并没有体验到那相同的狂喜。

欧班夫人想要给女儿最好的教育。既然居尤不能教她英语或音乐，她决定将女儿送往翁弗勒的乌尔苏拉修女学校。

维尔吉妮对此没有意见，但费莉西泰却很不开心，觉得夫人过于严厉了。然而，她还是接受了，毕竟这件事并不是她所能决定的，而她的女主人可能最了解情况。

有一天，一俩老旧的马车来到门外。车上下来一位修女，她是来接小姐的。费莉西泰将行李放在行李架上，向车夫叮嘱了几句，便将六罐果酱、一打梨子和一束紫罗兰放在车座上。

就在要离去时，维尔吉妮哭了。她紧紧抱着母亲，而母亲则亲吻她的额头，不断地对她说："好了，好了，我们得勇敢些！"步梯拉上来了，马车出发了。

马车走后，欧班夫人的情绪失控了。那天晚上，她所有的朋友，劳尔曼夫妇、勒沙普图瓦夫人、洛赫弗耶

姐妹、胡波维尔先生、布雷先生都来安慰她。

起初，女儿不在让她很伤心。但每周有三天，她都能收到女儿的信。其他几天，她则给女儿回信，在花园里散步、读书，以此打发时间。

每天早上，费莉西泰会习惯性地走进维尔吉妮的卧室，凝视着墙壁。她多想还能给她梳头，给她系鞋带，把她塞进被窝啊；多想能成天见到她那甜蜜的小脸蛋，握着她的手一起外出啊。为了找点事做，她试着做一些针线活儿。但她的手指太笨了，老是把线弄断。她没心思做任何事情，晚上也睡不着。她现在，用自己的话说，就是“体内空空的”。

为了能“有个伴儿”，她问欧班夫人能否允许她的外甥维克多过来看望。

维克多总在星期天弥撒过后那会儿来。他脸色红润，敞着胸，带着一股他刚刚走过的乡野的气息。她会立即为他摆好桌子。他们坐在桌子两头，面对面地吃午饭。为了节省开支，费莉西泰尽可能吃得少些，而维克多则吃很多，甚至吃到最后都睡着了。晚祷的钟声响了，她叫醒他，给他刷干净裤子，系好领带，然后靠在他的肩膀上，像一位自豪的母亲，向教堂走去。

他父母总是让他带点东西回去，一包糖、一块肥皂、一小瓶白兰地，有时甚至是钱。任何一件需要缝补的衣服，他都会带过来，而费莉西泰总是很乐意做这样的事情。一有机会，她就高兴地鼓励他再次过来。

八月里，维克多和他父亲一起到沿海一带捕鱼去了。

这时，暑假刚刚开始，孩子们回家了，这让费莉西泰有了些许的安慰。只是保罗变任性了，维尔吉妮也已大了，没法儿像对孩子那样待她了。这让他们之间的氛围变得尴尬，疏远。

维克多先后去了默尔克、敦刻尔克和布莱顿。每次航行回来，他都会带一份礼物给费莉西泰。第一次是贝壳做的盒子。第二次是一个咖啡杯。第三次是一个大大的姜饼人。他正长成一个英俊的年轻人。优美的身形，刚长出的一点胡髭，一副直爽开朗的表情，一顶总是戴在后脑勺上的小皮帽，让他看起来像是个领航员。为了逗费莉西泰高兴，他夹杂着水手的各种行话，给她讲故事。

一八一九年七月十四日，星期一（这是费莉西泰永远也不会忘记的日子），维克多说，他已签约受雇于一艘远洋轮船。两天后，他将从翁弗勒坐晚上的渡轮前往他的纵帆船，这艘船很快就会从勒阿弗尔启航。他这一去，

也许要两年。

想到要分别这么久，费莉西泰极为伤心。为了能与他最后告别，星期三晚上，在欧班夫人吃完饭后，她便从蓬莱韦克到翁弗勒，穿着木屐跑了十英里。

到各各他时，她没有朝左，而是向右走，结果在造船厂里迷了路，不得不原路返回。她向路人打听方向，那人告诉她得快点了。一路上，她绕着满是船只的海港走着，碰到了各种缆索。突然，她脚下的地面似乎倾斜了，光束呈十字形交织在眼前。她看到空中有几匹马，心想自己一定是疯了。

码头边，马群因害怕大海嘶鸣着。它们被起重架吊起，放到船里。船上人满为患，在苹果酒桶、奶酪筐和谷袋间拥挤着，走动着。母鸡在咯咯叫，船长在咒骂。甲板上，有个水手似乎对周遭的一切丝毫都不在意，靠着船头站着。费莉西泰没认出他，正一遍遍地叫着“维克多”。他抬起头，她向前冲来，但就在这时，舷梯突然从岸上被抽走了。

船只离了海港，被一群女人拖拽向前。她们在做事的时候，会齐声唱着歌。船体咯吱作响，沉重的波浪拍打着船头。然后船帆掉转，将所有人都遮挡在视线之外。

月光下，海面闪着银色的光泽，而航行其上的船看起来像是个黑点，越来越暗淡。最终，在远处被吞没，消失不见了。

回家的路上，途经各各他，费莉西泰突然想请求上帝怜悯所有她珍爱的人。她站在那里，祈祷了很长时间。她的双眼凝视着上方的云朵，眼泪滑落她的脸颊。整座城镇都睡了，除了那些海关的人。可以听见水从闸门的孔中流过，像是激流。钟声敲响了两点。

天亮前，女修道院是不会接待访客的。而费莉西泰也知道，如果她回来晚了，夫人肯定会很生气。因此，尽管她很想从维尔吉妮那儿得到一个小小的吻，但还是启程回家了。她踏进蓬莱韦克时，客栈的女仆才刚刚起床。

维克多太可怜了，他得在海浪上持续颠簸数月！她并不担忧他之前的航行，毕竟英格兰也好，布列塔尼也罢，都是可以回来的地方。但美洲，殖民地和安的列斯群岛，则迷失在世界另一边的未知领域里。

自他走后，费莉西泰无时不在想着她的外甥。天气炎热、阳光充足时，她担心他可能会渴了。暴风雨来临时，她害怕他可能会被雷电击中。听到风在烟囱里呼啸，将屋顶上的瓦片吹落，她则想象他正经受着同样的风暴，

正紧紧抓住折断的桅杆顶端，身子向后，被抛掷在大海的白沫之中。别的时候，受她所记得的地理书上那些插图的刺激，她想象他正在被野人吃掉，在树林里被猿猴捕获，或者正死在一片荒凉的海滩上。但她从未将这些焦虑告诉任何人。

欧班夫人则在担忧她的女儿。

修道院的修女说，她是个情感丰富的孩子，只是太过敏感。哪怕一点点的情感波动都会影响到她。这让她不得不放弃弹钢琴。

她母亲坚持要她定期写信。有一天早晨，邮差没有出现，她几乎不能自制，在房间里的扶手椅和窗户之间，来回走个不停。实在太过分了！都四天没消息了！

费莉西泰想到自己的境况可能对女主人有所安抚，便说：

“但是夫人，我已经六个月没有收到消息了。”

“谁的消息？”

“哎呀，我外甥的消息呀。”费莉西泰温柔地回答。

“哦，你的外甥！”欧班夫人耸耸肩，又在房间里踱起步来，那似乎在说：“我想都没想过他！他关我什么事呢！只不过是个小船员，一个乞丐。他不值得我焦虑。

但像我的女儿那样的……想想看！”

尽管自小就受尽虐待，但费莉西泰还是被欧班夫人深深伤害了。不过很快，她就平复了。

毕竟夫人为她的女儿心烦意乱，是可以理解的。

对费莉西泰来说，两个孩子是同等重要的。他们因她的爱而连接在一起。而让他们享有相同的命运，看起来也是恰当的。

费莉西泰听药剂师说，维克多的船已到了哈瓦那。他是在报纸上读到这则消息的。

由于与雪茄有关，费莉西泰幻想着哈瓦那是这样的一个地方：人们除了抽烟，什么都不干。她想象着维克多正走在一群黑鬼之间，被烟雾笼罩着。“如果需要的话”，从哈瓦那可以走回来吗？那里离蓬莱韦克有多远？为此，她去请教了布雷先生。

他找来地图册，开始解说经纬线。费莉西泰听蒙了。布雷先生坐在她前面，沾沾自喜，好像他无所不知似的。最后，他拿出铅笔，在地图上一个椭圆形斑点的缺口处，指了指一个几乎看不见的黑点说：“就是这里了。”费莉西泰凑近看着地图。这些彩色的线条组成的网络压迫着她的双眼，但并没有告诉她任何事情。布雷先生问，她

在迷惑什么。她说，他是否可以指出维克多现在住的房子。布雷先生举起手臂，打了个喷嚏，哈哈大笑，被自己遇到头脑如此简单的人逗乐了。费莉西泰没能理解他的笑点。毕竟，她理解力有限，她甚至期望能在那里看到一张她外甥的照片呢。

两周后，是里埃巴照常去集市的日子。他走进厨房，递给费莉西泰一封她姐夫的信。两人都不识字，费莉西泰只好拿给女主人看。

欧班夫人正在数一件织物的针脚。她将活儿放在一边，打开信，停顿了片刻，然后低沉着声音，严肃地说："他们给你带来了……坏消息。你外甥……"

维克多死了。这就是那封信所说的。

费莉西泰倒在了椅子上，头抵着墙，眼皮紧闭，眼眶泛红。她僵在那儿，低垂着头，双手无力地垂在身旁，凝视前方，一遍遍地重复说："可怜的孩子！可怜的孩子！"

里埃巴站在那里，看着她，叹了口气。欧班夫人轻轻颤抖。

她建议费莉西泰到特鲁维尔去看看她姐姐。

费莉西泰做了个手势，意思是那没有必要。

一片沉默。里埃巴老头觉得他最好离开。

他走后，费莉西泰说："他们是不会在意的，一点都不会。"

她再次低头，坐在那儿，不时心烦意乱地玩弄着摆在桌上的编织针。

院子里走过一群女人，正推着一车湿漉漉的亚麻衣服。

透过窗户，费莉西泰看见了她们，突然想起要洗的衣服。昨天她用碱液泡过，今天该洗出来了。于是，她起身出了房间。

她的洗衣板和木盆都在图克河边。她将一堆内衣扔到岸边，卷起袖子，抓住棒槌。这捶打的声响，在邻居的花园里都能听到。牧场空落无人，风吹皱了河面。河床上长长的水草，随波漂流着，像死人的头发在水里向下漂移。费莉西泰很勇敢，克制着她的悲痛，一直到天黑。但当她独自一人在房间里时，还是没能忍住。她平躺在床垫上，将脸埋在枕头里，用拳头挤压着太阳穴。

很久以后，她从那艘船的船长那里得知维克多死时的情况。他得了黄热病，在医院里放了很多血。四个医生同时在给他治疗，而他立即死了。主治医生说："上帝啊，又死了一个。"

维克多一直受父母苛待。费莉西泰不再乐意见到他

们。他们也没有去联系费莉西泰。可能他们只是把她忘了，也可能是因为贫穷让他们生就了一副硬心肠。

维尔吉妮越来越虚弱了。

呼吸困难，咳嗽持续，高烧不断，脸上布满暗淡的红疹，所有这些都在显示某种隐晦的身心失调。普帕特医生建议她去普罗旺斯度假。欧班夫人听从了他的意见。如果不是蓬莱韦克的天气不好，她会立即将维尔吉妮接回家的。

她和一个出租马车的人达成协议，让他每周二带她去往修道院。修道院的花园里有一座露台，可以俯瞰塞纳河。维尔吉妮靠着母亲的手臂，踩着掉落的葡萄叶，上下来回地散步。她会望着远处的帆船，以及从唐卡维尔的别墅到勒阿弗尔的灯塔这一带的海岸。有时，太阳突然穿破云层，照得她直眨眼睛。之后，她们会坐在棚架下休息。她母亲弄来一小杯上等的马拉加葡萄酒。维尔吉妮会喝那么两口，一想到自己会喝醉就发笑。

她开始恢复元气。秋天缓慢地滑过。费莉西泰竭尽所能安慰欧班夫人。但有一天傍晚，她在镇里办完差事回来，发现普帕特医生的马车停在门前。普帕特医生在大厅出口处，欧班夫人在系她的帽子。

“把我的脚炉、钱包和手套拿来，快！”

维尔吉妮患了肺炎，夫人怕她好不了。

“我确信没那么糟糕。”医生说。于是，两人一起爬上了他的马车。四周落着慌乱的雪。夜晚正在来临，天气异常寒冷。

费莉西泰猛冲进教堂，点了一支蜡烛后，就去追赶普帕特医生的马车了。过了整整一小时，她从后头跳上来，紧紧抓住马车的边。突然，她想起来：“院门没有关！万一小偷进来怎么办？”于是，她又从车里跳回了路上。

第二天，在最初的日光中，她来到医生家。医生回来过，但又去乡下探望病人了。她在客栈里等着，想着有人可能会捎信过来。最终，在早晨的朦胧光线里，她坐上了利雪来的公共马车。

修道院坐落在一条陡窄的街道底部。她从半途往下走时，听到修道院里传来的奇怪声响。那是丧钟的鸣响。“那一定是为别人敲的。”她想着，大声地叩着门环。

不久，她听到有脚步声拖拽而来，门开了些许，一个修女出现了。

这位善良的修女庄重地宣称“她刚过世”。就在这时，

圣里奥纳多教堂的钟声响起，越发显得响亮。

费莉西泰来到三楼。

在门口，她看到维尔吉妮仰卧着，双手紧握，嘴巴张着，头向后仰。头上方，一尊黑色的受难像向她倾斜而来。她的脸，比她周边僵直地垂挂下来的帘子还要惨白。欧班夫人躺在那里，抱着床脚，疯狂地啜泣。院长站在她右边。三支蜡烛在五斗柜上闪着小小的红色光圈。外面，雾气蒙上了窗玻璃。几位修女来了，带走了欧班夫人。

整整两个晚上，费莉西泰都没有离开维尔吉妮的床边。她坐在那儿，不断重复着相同的祷词。她起身，将圣水洒在被单上，又回到椅子里，继续凝视这位死去的姑娘。第一天守夜结束时，她注意到她的脸变黄了，嘴唇变蓝了，鼻子变瘦了，而她的眼睛也凹陷了下来。不止一次，她亲吻她的眼睛。此时，如果维尔吉妮再次睁开眼，她也不会有丝毫的惊讶。对她这样的人来说，超自然的事情是很平常的。她将她放好，给她穿上寿衣，放入棺材，给她戴上花环，将她的头发铺展开来。她的头发很美，对她这个年龄的女孩来说，算是长的了。费莉西泰剪下一大卷头发，将其中一半放进怀中，打定主

意，永不分离。

按欧班夫人的意思，人们将尸体运回了蓬莱韦克。欧班夫人坐在关得严实的马车里，尾随着灵车。

葬礼弥撒过后，要过三刻钟才能到达公墓。保罗领着队伍，哭泣着。布雷先生在他后面，随后是蓬莱韦克的各个名流，以及戴着黑面纱哭泣的女人，最后是费莉西泰。费莉西泰不禁想起她的外甥。想到不能给他这最后的荣耀，她感到了双重的悲伤，就好像他正随着维尔吉妮一同被埋葬了。

欧班夫人绝望了。

起初，她反抗上帝，认为他将维尔吉妮从她身边带走是不公正的，因为她从未做过错事，也没有什么事能让她内疚。然而，也许是有的。她应该带她去南方。别的医生会治好她。她自我谴责，希望能随女儿而去，并在睡梦中痛苦地呼叫。有一个梦特别折磨她。她的丈夫，打扮得像一个水手，从漫长的旅途归来，流着泪，哽咽着说，他收到指示，要带维尔吉妮走。接着，他们绞尽脑汁，想给她找一个躲藏的地方。

有一次，她失魂落魄地从花园回来。就在这之前（她指着一个地方），父亲和女儿依次出现在她面前。他们什

么也没做，只是望着她。

有好几个月，她都待在房间里，无精打采的。费莉西泰温柔地劝说她，要她好好照顾自己，为了她的儿子，她过世的丈夫，以及出于对“她”的怀念。

“她？”欧班夫人说着，仿佛从睡梦中醒来。“哦，是的，你当然没有忘记她，你有吗？”她说的是公墓，那是欧班夫人绝不会去的地方。

费莉西泰每天都去那儿。

四点的钟声一响，她便走过一排房子，爬上山，打开门，来到维尔吉妮的墓前。墓上立着一根粉色的大理石柱，底下是块石板，一条链子将四周围成一个小花园。繁花几乎要淹没那张独立的花床了。费莉西泰给叶子浇水，换上新的沙子，然后趴在地上，除尽地面的杂草。如果欧班夫人最终能来，她会从中找到安慰，一种对痛失所爱的慰藉。

多年过去了，年岁间极为相似，无非是来来去去的年度教堂节日：复活节、圣母升天节、万圣节。反倒是日常中那些微小的事件，在数年后，会让她们想起某些特殊的日子。例如，一八二五年，两个装玻璃的工人粉刷过堂；一八二七年，屋顶的一部分掉落在院子里，差

点砸死了路人；一八二八年夏天，轮到夫人给教区居民发放祝圣面包，差不多就在这时，布雷先生神秘地离开了镇子。然后，一个接一个地，相识的熟人都离开了：居尤、里埃巴、勒沙普图瓦夫人、罗贝林，以及她那已瘫痪多年的老叔叔格莱芒维特。

有一晚，邮车的车夫来到蓬莱韦克，带来“七月革命”的消息。几天后，新的县长上任了：勒森尼耶男爵，曾经的美洲领事。他来到蓬莱韦克，带着他的妻子，以及他的小姨和三位年纪很大的小姐。人们经常看见她们，穿着飘逸的长罩衣，出现在她们家的草坪上。她们还有一个黑人仆从和一只鹦鹉。她们拜访欧班夫人，以表达敬意。她也回访。只要远远看见，费莉西泰就会跑来告诉欧班夫人，说她们已在路上了。但能唤起欧班夫人兴趣的只有一件事，那就是她儿子的来信。

他看似无法专注于任何事情，整日沉湎于酒馆。欧班夫人会支付他的账单，但新的账单很快就来了。她在窗旁织着毛衣，发出沉重的叹息。即使身在厨房摇着手纺车的费莉西泰也能听到。

两个女人经常一起沿着花园的格子墙漫步。她们仍会频繁地谈起维尔吉妮，想着她是否会喜欢某某事，或

她对某某场合会说些什么。

她所有的东西仍保存在儿童房卧室的橱柜里。欧班夫人尽量避免往里查看。但在夏日的一天，她终究没能忍住，打开了。橱柜里飞出了好多蛾子。

维尔吉妮的连衣裙成排地挂在架子下，上面摆着三个玩偶、一些发箍、一副玩偶的家具和她的洗手盆。两个女人拿出所有的裙子、袜子和手帕，平铺在两张床上，再叠起来。这些可怜的东西躺在那儿，在一束阳光的照耀下，显出了所有的污渍，以及因维尔吉妮的身体运动弄出来的折痕。空气温暖，天空湛蓝，一只黑鸟在外面鸣唱，整个世界显得格外平和。她们找到一顶栗色的长毛绒帽，但已被飞蛾蛀蚀了。费莉西泰问是否可以将它作为纪念品留下来。两个女人看着彼此，双眼满是泪水。欧班夫人张开双臂，费莉西泰扑了过去。女主人和仆人相互拥抱着，在一个不分贵贱的吻里，联结起她们的悲伤。

她们是第一次这样做，之前从未发生过。因为就其天性而言，欧班夫人是非常矜持的。费莉西泰从未如此感激她，仿佛得了一份无价的礼物。自此之后，她更为溺爱女主人，像狗一般忠贞，像对待圣人一般虔诚。

随着时间的流逝，她本性中的善意越发凸显了。

有一天，她听到街上行军的鼓声，便站在门前，捧着一壶苹果酒，递给士兵喝。她帮着看护霍乱病人，照顾波兰的难民。有一个波兰人甚至说，想要娶她，但他们发生了很严重的争执。那是在一天早晨，她做完礼拜回来，发现他坐在她的厨房里，镇定自若地吃着一盘色拉，而那是她为午饭准备的。

波兰人走后，她注意到了一个叫考尔米克的老人。传言他在一七九三年做过很残暴的事情。现在他住在河边一间破败的猪圈里。镇里的小孩经常从墙缝里窥看他，朝他扔石子。他躺在草垫上，咳得快呛住了。他有一头披散的长发，眼皮发炎了，手臂上长着一个比他的头还大的瘤子。费莉西泰给了他一些布，竭力打扫干净他简陋的住所。她甚至想，也许可以将他安置在外屋，一处不会打扰到夫人的地方。瘤子破了，她就每天都给他换衣服。有时，她会给他带来一小片蛋糕，或扶他出去，将他放在一捆麦秆上，晒晒太阳。这个贫穷可怜的人语无伦次，颤动着，以一种几乎听不见的低语感谢她，说害怕她走掉。见她要走，就会伸出双手。他死了，费莉西泰做了一场弥撒，让他的灵魂安息。

同一天，她收到一份极为美妙的惊喜。在她吃饭时，勒森尼耶夫人的黑人仆从来了，带着一只关在笼子里的鹦鹉，还有栖木、链子和挂锁。男爵夫人给欧班夫人带来一张字条，说她丈夫荣升省长了，晚上他们就要离开蓬莱韦克。她问欧班夫人，能否发善心收下这只鹦鹉，作为她们友谊的纪念，以及她表达敬意的象征。

很长一段时间，费莉西泰对这只鹦鹉心存好奇。因为它来自美洲，一个总能让她想起她的维克多的地方。她曾就这只鸟问过仆从。有一次，她甚至说“夫人若能照料它，会很开心的”。

黑人仆从就把这事说给他的女主人，而她反正也不能带走，于是很乐意抓住这次机会，将它脱手了。

四

这只鹦鹉叫露露。他的身子是绿色的，翼尖是粉色的，额头是蓝色的，而胸脯是金色的。

不幸的是，他有着很惹人厌的习惯：咬栖木，拔羽毛，到处抛洒粪便，还将杯里的水飞溅得满笼子都是。欧班夫人被惹怒了，就把他送给费莉西泰来照料。

她决心教他说话，而且没过多久，他便会说：‘好孩子！’‘您的仆人，先生！’‘万福玛利亚！’她把他放在正门附近，路过的人都很惊奇，因为他竟对“波利”没有反应，而所有的鹦鹉都叫这个名字。有人说他更像火鸡，有人则叫他傻瓜。费莉西泰觉得这些嘲弄太伤人了。令人惊奇的是，露露有种奇怪的执拗：有人看他就拒绝说话。

但他无疑还是喜欢有人陪伴的。星期天，当洛赫弗耶姐妹、胡波维尔先生，欧班夫人的新朋友药剂师翁弗洛瓦、瓦林先生和马修船长来玩纸牌的时候，露露就会用翅膀拍打窗玻璃，发出剧烈的骚乱声，闹得人都无法听清在说什么。

显然，他觉得布雷先生的脸很可笑。一见到他，就会忍不住爆发出一阵笑声。他粗砺的声音回荡在院子四周。邻居们听到后，就会来到窗前，也随之大笑。为了不让他看见，布雷先生会将脸藏在帽子后面，沿着墙偷偷地走过房前。他走过河边，从后花园绕进屋里。他投向这只鸟的眼神，可不是很温柔的。

肉铺的伙计在露露想偷吃他篮子里的东西时，弹了弹他的脑门儿。自那以后，露露总想隔着衬衫啄他。于是，法布威胁说要扭断他的脖子。他倒不是天性残忍，

只是手臂上的文身和那长长的络腮胡，可能会给人留下这样的印象。事实上，他很喜欢这只鹦鹉。为了逗乐，甚至想教他脏话。费莉西泰怕他沾上这些坏毛病，就把他移到了厨房里。链子也被拿掉了，他可以在房子里四处逗留。

下楼的时候，他会用嘴钩子顶在前面的台阶上，抬起右脚，接着是左脚。费莉西泰总担心这些奇怪的动作，会将鹦鹉弄晕。果然，他生病了，不能说话，不能吃东西。他的舌尖下生了溃疡，有时候母鸡也会得这种病。费莉西泰用指甲戳破他嘴里的肿块，治好了他。有一天，保罗少爷愚蠢地将雪茄烟喷到他的鼻子里。还有一次，劳尔曼夫人用伞尖逗弄他，他咬掉了金属箍。后来，他就不见了。

费莉西泰将他放在草地上，让他呼吸新鲜空气，然后便回了室内一会儿。回来时，鹦鹉就不见了。她在灌木丛、河边，甚至在屋顶上找着，也不顾女主人喊着说："小心，你一定是疯啦！"随后，她找遍了蓬莱韦克的每一座花园，遇到路人就问："你凑巧见过我的鹦鹉吗？"对不熟悉鹦鹉的人，她还会做一番详细的描述。突然，她似乎看到一个绿色的东西在山脚下的磨坊后面飞着。

可到了山顶，却什么也没有。一个小贩说，不久前，他在圣梅兰区西蒙老夫人的店里见过它。费莉西泰就一路跑去，但没人知道她在说什么。最后，她回来了，精疲力竭，鞋子磨破了，意志消沉。她坐在花园的椅子中央，挨着夫人，说着她所做的事情。这时，有什么轻柔地落在肩上。是露露！他究竟去干吗了？也许只是绕着镇子走了走。

费莉西泰没能立即从惊吓中复原。如果知道真相，也可以说，她再也不能恢复了。

因为着凉，她患上了扁桃体炎。不久，耳朵也疼了。三年后，她全聋了，说话特别大声，即使在教堂里也是。她的罪过散播在教区的各个角落，即使这并非有损她的名声，也不冒犯他人，但神父仍然觉得，听她忏悔最好在圣器室内。

头脑中想象的嗡嗡声令她备受折磨。她的女主人经常说：“天啊，你多蠢啊！”费莉西泰会回答说：“是的，夫人。”然后，她四处打量，仍想要找寻这嘈杂声是哪里发出的。

她陷入越来越小的自我世界里。教堂的钟声、牧场上的牛哞，永远地离她而去了。所有的活物都如鬼魂，

从旁静默地经过。现在唯一能抵达她耳朵的声音，便是鹦鹉的叫声。

像是有意给她解闷似的，他模仿起烤肉叉转动的咔嗒响、鱼贩子尖锐的叫声，或者街对面工匠的锯齿声。无论何时，门铃一响起来，他就会模仿欧班夫人说：“费莉西泰，门，门！”

他们彼此交谈。鹦鹉不断地重复着三个烂熟的短句。而费莉西泰呢，则用没什么意义但发自肺腑的话来回答。在她孤绝的世界里，露露几乎成了她的儿子，她溺爱他。而他则爬上她的手指，咬咬她的唇，挂在她的披肩上。有时，她的脸会挨着他的，摇晃着，就像护士对婴儿做的那样。帽子的两翼和鸟的翅膀一起颤动着。

乌云聚集，雷电轰隆作响的时候，鹦鹉就大声地叫着，显然是忆起了野生森林里的暴雨。下雨的声音，让他很不安。他满屋子疯狂地飞着，撞上天花板，撞倒了所有的东西，最后穿过窗户逃到花园里，泼溅着泥水。但他很快就会回来，高高地栖息在壁炉架上，跳上跳下的，晾干了羽毛，自豪地展示着他的尾巴或者嘴。

一八三七年那个可怕的冬日，有一天早晨，她见天冷，就把他放在壁炉旁。这时，她发现他死在了笼子里。

头下垂着，爪子抓着金属门闩。想必是死于中风吧，但费莉西泰却想，他可能吃了欧芹，毒发而死。尽管没有确切的证据，但她怀疑是法布干的。

她哭得很伤心，最终女主人说："为什么不把他做成标本呢？"

费莉西泰咨询了药剂师，他对鹦鹉一向很好。

他写信到勒阿弗尔，一个叫弗拉切的接了这份活儿。考虑到公共马车有时会丢失包裹，费莉西泰决定亲自带着鹦鹉，前往翁弗勒。

道路向前延伸，两旁是无尽的苹果树，光秃秃的，没什么叶子。水沟里结着冰。她走过农场时，狗吠叫着。她的手缩在斗篷下方，篮子挂在手臂上。费莉西泰穿着黑色小木屐，在路中央快步走着。

她穿过树林，走过上歇纳，最终来到了圣加蒂安。

这时，在她身后起了一团尘土，只见一辆邮车飓风似的，从山上疾驰而来。车夫看女人没有躲开的意思，便站起身，目光越过马车顶，朝外望去。他和车童都竭力叫喊着。他想让四匹马停下，但没有用。它们反而越来越快，朝着她奔来。他们经过时，前头的两匹马蹭过了费莉西泰。车夫猛地一拉缰绳，迫使马匹转向了路旁。

盛怒之下，他举起手臂，挥鞭打去，从她的脸一直打到了上半身。她仰面倒在了地上。

醒来时，她所做的第一件事，就是看看篮子。还好，露露毫发无损。她觉得右脸一阵阵地灼痛，便用手摸了摸，看见手是血红色的。她正在流血。

她坐在石堆上，用手帕轻抚着脸，然后吃了点预先备好的面包。她看着鹦鹉，试图借此忘记伤口。

到了埃屈埃莫维尔的山顶，她便看见翁弗勒像是群星般闪烁的夜间灯火。再过去便是大海，朦胧地延展向远方。突然，她感到一阵晕眩。悲惨的童年，初恋带来的失望之情，外甥的离世，维尔吉妮的亡故，所有这些都潮水似的，汹涌袭来，涌进她的体内，让她窒息。

她坚持要和船长当面说话，要他好好照顾这个包裹，尽管她没说这里面有什么。

弗拉切拖了很长时间，尽管他总说下周就会寄出来。六个月后，他才说将箱子寄出来了，但之后就再没有下文了。费莉西泰怕露露再也不会回来。她想："他被偷了，我知道的。"

最终，他还是来了。他看起来也很棒，栖息在一根树枝上，用螺丝钉固定在桃木底座上。他抬着一只爪，

头侧向一边，嘴里叼着一颗坚果。标本师为了添加一点华丽的质感，还给坚果镀了金。

费莉西泰将他安置在房间里。

她很少让人进入这个房间，里面放着各种宗教小摆件和杂七杂八的东西，像是小教堂，又像是集市。

门旁有个大衣橱，妨碍人开门。面向花园的窗户对面，有一扇能望见院子的圆形小窗。有一张没有弹簧的、朴素的床。床旁边是一张桌子，桌上放着一个水壶、两把梳子、一个带缺口的碟子——上面放着一小块蓝色的肥皂。墙上挂着念珠、纪念章、几幅圣母像、一个椰子壳做的圣水杯。五斗橱蒙着布，像是圣坛，上面放着维克多给她的贝壳盒子，还有一把喷壶、一个球、一些练习册、一本带插图的地理书和一双小小的短筒靴。镜子的挂钉上，挂着那顶小小的长绒帽！这些纪念品，对费莉西泰来说，都有着很深的意义。她甚至连老爷的一件礼服都留着。欧班夫人不要的东西，她都在房间里找地方放着，像五斗橱旁放着人造花，天窗里挂着阿图瓦伯爵的画像。

至于露露，则放在专为他准备的小木架上。那木架被固定在面向房间凸起的壁炉侧墙上。每天早上醒来时，

她都会在晨光中看见他。她会想起那些过去的日子，那些微小的事件，直至想到各种细枝末节。想起这些，并不让她感到悲伤，反而充满了平静。

由于不能和人交流，她的生活像是在梦游。唯有圣体瞻礼节的游行，似乎还能将她带回到生活里来。她拜访邻居，收集烛台和垫子，用来装饰那些一般会放在街上的圣坛。

她来到教堂，坐下来，凝视着圣灵的画像。她发现圣灵和她的鹦鹉很像。这种相像在一幅埃皮纳勒版画上表现得尤为明显，上面画着我主受洗的情景。那鸽子有着深红的翅膀、祖母绿的身体，跟露露一模一样。费莉西泰将这幅画买回来，挂在阿图瓦伯爵画像挂的地方，这样她就能同时看到它们。在她的心中，两者联结在了一起。因着与圣灵的联结，鹦鹉更神圣了；而圣灵也因此更显生动，更有意义。上帝当然不会选中一只鸽子去言说，因为鸽子不能说话。那么，一定会选露露的先祖吧。费莉西泰望着圣灵那幅画祈祷时，不时会微微转头，看着鹦鹉。

她想过加入圣女姐妹团，但被欧班夫人劝阻了。

现在，发生了一件大事——保罗结婚了。

起先，他是法庭书记员，随后他去经商，在海关工作，在税务局做事，甚至还考虑过加入森林和水利部门。到了三十六岁时，仿佛受了神启似的，他突然发现了自己的天职——登记处办公室！事实上，他已展现出了这方面的天赋。一位检查官已将女儿许配给他，并答应动用他的影响力，助他晋升。

他正严肃地履行自己的职责，带她来见母亲。

她指摘蓬莱韦克的所有事情，期望自己能像皇族一样被人对待。她伤害费莉西泰甚深。见她走了，欧班夫人顿觉松了口气。

接下来的那周，她们听闻布雷先生死在了下布列塔尼的一家客栈里。谣传说，他是自杀的。很快，这就被证实了。人们开始质疑他的正直。欧班夫人检查她的账本，发现了一系列他的不法行为：盗用应收租金、没有申报树木所得、伪造收据，等等。他还有一个私生子，与“多聚莱的某人有着不正当的关系”。

欧班夫人很难过。一八五三年三月，她觉得胸口疼痛。舌头上覆着层灰色的苔衣。几次放血治疗都没能减轻她的呼吸困难。到了第九晚，她就死了，刚好七十二岁。

人们觉得她看起来要年轻些，因为她的头发是黑色

的，还一束束地垂在两旁，裹着她苍白的麻脸。没什么朋友来哀悼她。她平素傲慢，让人对她保持了距离。

费莉西泰哭了，很少有仆人像她那样为主人哭。夫人先于她去世，让她怎么也想不通，觉得这违背了事物的自然秩序。无法接受，也不真实。

十天后，也就是从贝桑松赶来所费的时间，继承人来到了现场。欧班夫人的媳妇翻开了所有的抽屉，留了一些家具，剩下的全卖掉了。随后，他们便返回了登记处办公室。

欧班夫人的扶手椅、小桌子、暖脚炉和八张椅子都被运走了！墙上的画像也被拿掉了，只留下一块黄色的空当。他们还带走了两张小孩的床和床垫，以及橱柜里维尔吉妮的东西。费莉西泰在房间之间来回走着，心都碎了。

第二天，门上贴着一张告示。药剂师对着她的耳朵大声说，房子要卖掉了。

费莉西泰一阵晕眩，坐了下来。

一想到要搬出自己的房间，她就极为不安。对可怜的露露来说，那也是再合适不过的地方了。她满怀痛苦，凝视着他，祈求圣灵帮助。她跪在鹦鹉面前祈祷，养成了崇拜偶像的习惯。有时候，阳光透过小窗，落在鹦鹉

的玻璃眼珠上，散发着明亮的光，将她带入了狂喜之中。

女主人给费莉西泰留了一笔三百八十法郎的退休金。花园可以供给她蔬菜。至于衣服，足够她穿到生命中的最后一刻。为了节省灯火，天一黑，她就上床睡觉。

她不怎么出门，免得走过二手商店时看见正摆着的那些旧家具。自被摔晕后，她就拖着一条腿走路。现在，她更虚弱了。最近，西蒙老夫人的杂货店破产了，她每天早晨都来为她劈柴打水。

她的视力越来越差。百叶窗也不再打开了。一晃多年，没人来租房子，也没人来买。

费莉西泰怕被人赶走，从未让人来修房子。屋顶的木板条烂了，整个冬天，雨水打湿了她的长枕头。复活节过去不久，她咯血了。

西蒙老夫人叫来一位医生。费莉西泰想知道她怎么了，但她的耳朵全聋了，很难听到他们说什么，只捕捉到一个词:“肺炎”。她是知道这个词的。她平静地回答说:“哈！跟夫人一样。”跟随夫人的脚步，她觉得这很自然。

准备圣坛的日子临近了。

第一座圣坛照例放在山脚下，第二座在邮局外面，第三座在街道的半途。最后一座该放在哪儿，起了些争

执，但教区的女人们最终同意放在欧班夫人的院子里。

费莉西泰呼吸更艰难了，发烧也更严重。不能为圣坛做点什么，让她很难过。至少她得在上面放点什么吧。于是，她想到了鹦鹉。邻居们反对说，这样并不合适，但神父却允许了。这让费莉西泰很快乐，要神父收下她唯一的财产露露，作为死前送出的礼物。

从星期二到星期六，圣体瞻礼节前夕，她的咳嗽加剧。到了晚上，脸绷得紧紧的，嘴唇粘着牙床。她开始呕吐。第二天一早，天蒙蒙亮，她感觉很不好，便请求见神父。临终涂油礼时，四周站着三位善良的女人。然后，她说要和法布谈谈。

法布穿着他星期天最好的衣服来了。如此忧伤的氛围，令他很不舒服。

“请你原谅我。”她说着，用力朝他伸出手臂，“我还以为是你杀了他。”

她在说什么废话？她怎能怀疑像他这样的人是一个凶手！法布很生气，忍不住要发脾气。

“她头脑迷糊了，”她们说，“你肯定能看得出来。”

费莉西泰似乎不时地在同幽灵谈话。女人们走了，只有西蒙老夫人留了下来，在吃午饭。

不久，她拿来露露，靠近费莉西泰。“来吧，”她说，“和他道别。”

露露不是尸体，但也被蛆蛀食了。一只翅膀断了，填充物从肚子里露了出来。但费莉西泰眼睛已瞎，没能看到。她亲吻他的额头，让他贴着自己的脸颊。西蒙老夫人将他从她那里拿开，重新放在了圣坛上。

五

从牧场那里飘来夏日的气息。苍蝇在空中嗡嗡作响。阳光在河面闪耀，照暖了屋顶上的石板瓦。西蒙老夫人回了房间，正轻柔地打着盹睡去。

突然，她被钟声惊醒了。人们正做完晚祷出来。费莉西泰镇静了许多。她想到了游行，清晰地看到了所有的一切，仿佛就置身于其中。

所有的小学生、唱诗班和消防员，都走在了人行道上。街道中央，走在队伍前头的，是执戟的教堂守卫、捧着大十字架的教区执事、管理男孩的学校校长，以及母亲般盯着女孩的修女。三个最可爱的女孩，像头发卷曲的天使，正将玫瑰花瓣撒向空中。在她们身后，助祭

张开双臂，正指挥着乐队；两个捧香炉的，每走一步，都会转过头看着圣体。圣体由穿着华丽长袍的神父捧着，由四个教区委员在其上举着顶红色的天鹅绒华盖护佑。在路上，在挂着白布的房墙之间，一大群人尾随而来，最终来到山脚下。

费莉西泰额前直冒冷汗。西蒙老夫人用布给她擦拭，对自己说，终有一天她也会这样走的。

人群的嘈杂声越来越响，有一瞬间特别响亮，然后又消退了。

一阵枪声震得窗户嗡嗡作响。那是骑马的人正在向圣体匣致敬。费莉西泰转动眼珠，费力地问："他还好吗？"她还在担心鹦鹉。

费莉西泰正进入她的弥留时刻。她喘着气，短促而嘶哑，两肋艰难地起伏，嘴角聚集着泡沫，全身开始颤抖。

外面，街上传来乐器的嘟嘟声、孩子响亮的声音，以及男人低沉的声响。有那么一些时刻，一切都沉寂了，能听到脚步因散落的花瓣变得轻柔，像是羊群穿过牧场。

神职人员走进院子。西蒙老夫人爬上椅子，朝小窗外张望，正好能看到窗下的圣坛。

圣坛挂着绿色花环，镶着英式针织的花边。正中间

有一个小小的方盒子，放着圣人的遗物。两边各有一棵橘子树。沿着圣坛摆放的是一排银烛台、瓷花瓶。花瓶里插着向日葵、百合、牡丹、毛地黄和绣球花。这串绚烂的色彩，从圣坛高处一路向下，延展至铺在鹅卵石上方的毯子。花丛里，可以见到其他一些珍贵的装饰品：一个装饰着紫罗兰花环的镀银糖罐，在小片青苔上闪烁的阿朗松宝石耳坠，两扇描画着风景的中国屏风。露露掩藏在玫瑰花底下，只见到他额头上的那点蓝，像块青金石。

教区委员、唱诗班、小孩在院子的三面站好。神父缓缓走来，将那大大的闪光的球体放在圣坛的花边上。所有人都跪了下来，一片沉静。香炉随链子晃动来回摇摆着。

一道蓝色的烟升起，进入费莉西泰的房间。她张大鼻孔，以一种神秘的狂热品味着。随后，她闭上眼睛，唇间现出一抹微笑。她的心跳放慢了，越来越微弱、模糊，像泉水干涸，回音消逝。就在呼出最后一口气时，她仿佛看到，天国开启的地方，一只巨大的鹦鹉在头上徘徊，来接纳她。

企鹅经典：小黑书　第一辑

01. 贝尔科洛蕾夫人与神父

[意] 薄伽丘

02. 泄密的心

[美] 爱伦·坡

03. 醋栗

[俄] 契诃夫

04. 一个人需要许多土地吗?

[俄] 列夫·托尔斯泰

05. 一颗简单的心

[法] 福楼拜

06. 傻子的一生

[日] 芥川龙之介

07. 萎缩的胳膊

[英] 托马斯·哈代

08. 樱花树下的清酒

[日] 吉田兼好

09. 虎！虎！

[英] 威廉·布莱克

10. 给一个青年诗人的十封信

[奥] 里尔克

Penguin Little Black Classics Vol. I

01. GIOVANNI BOCCACCIO
Mrs Rosie and the Priest

02. EDGAR ALLAN POE
The Tell-Tale Heart

03. ANTON CHEKHOV
Gooseberries

04. LEO TOLSTOY
How Much Land Does a Man Need?

05. GUSTAVE FLAUBERT
A Simple Heart

06. RYUNOSUKE AKUTAGAWA
The Life of a Stupid Man

07. THOMAS HARDY
The Withered Arm

08. KENKO
A Cup of Sake Beneath the Cherry Trees

09. WILLIAM BLAKE
Tyger Tyger

10. RAINER MARIA RILKE
Letters to a Young Poet

‘If I stopped now, after coming all this way – well, they’d call me an idiot!’

LEO TOLSTOY

How Much Land Does A Man Need?

Translated by
Ronald Wilks

Contents

How Much Land Does A Man Need?

1

An elder sister came from the town to visit her younger sister in the country. This elder sister was married to a merchant and the younger to a peasant in the village. The two sisters sat down for a talk over a cup of tea and the elder started boasting about the superiority of town life, with all its comforts, the fine clothes her children wore, the exquisite food and drink, the skating, parties and visits to the theatre.

The younger sister resented this and in turn scoffed at the life of a merchant's wife and sang the praises of her own life as a peasant.

'I wouldn't care to change my life for yours,' she said. 'I admit mine is dull, but at least we have no worries. You live in grander style, but you must do a great deal of business or you'll be ruined. You know the proverb, "Loss is Gain's elder brother." One day you are rich and the next you might find yourself out in the street. Here in the country we don't have those ups and downs. A peasant's life may be poor, but it's long. Although we may never be rich, we'll always have enough to eat.'

Then the elder sister said her piece.

'Enough to eat indeed with nothing but those filthy pigs and calves! What do you know about nice clothes and good manners! However hard your good husband slaves away you'll spend your lives in the muck and that's where you'll die. And the same goes for your children.'

'Well, what of it?' the younger sister retorted. 'That's how it is here. But at least we know where we are. We don't have to crawl to anyone and we're afraid of no one. But you in the town are surrounded by temptations. All may be well one day, the next the Devil comes along and tempts your husband with cards, women and drink. And then you're ruined. It does happen, doesn't it?'

Pakhom, the younger sister's husband, was lying over the stove listening to the women's chatter.

'It's true what you say,' he said. 'Take me. Ever since I was a youngster I've been too busy tilling the soil to let that kind of nonsense enter my head. My only grievance is that I don't have enough land. Give me enough of that and I'd fear no one – not even the Devil himself!'

The sisters finished their tea, talked a little longer about dresses, cleared away the tea things and went to bed.

But the Devil had been sitting behind the stove and had heard everything. He was delighted that a peasant's wife had led her husband to boast that if he had enough land he would fear no one, not even the Devil. 'Good!' he thought. 'I'll have a little game with you. I shall see that you have plenty of land and that way I'll get you in my clutches!'

2

Not far from the village lived a lady with a small estate of about three hundred acres. She had always been on good terms with the peasants and had never ill-treated them. But then she had taken on an old soldier to manage her estate and he proceeded to harass the peasants by constantly imposing fines. No matter how careful Pakhom was, one of his horses might stray into the lady's oats, or a cow might sometimes wander into her garden, or some calves might venture out on to her meadows. Every time this happened he would have to pay a fine.

Pakhom would pay up and then he would go and swear at his family and beat them. All that summer Pakhom had to put up with a great deal from that manager, so he welcomed winter when it came and his cattle had to be kept in the shed: although he begrudged the fodder, at least he wouldn't have to worry about them straying.

That winter word got round that the lady wanted to sell some of her land and that the innkeeper on the highway was trying to agree on a price with her. The peasants took this news very badly. 'If that innkeeper gets his hands on that land he'll start slapping even more fines on us than that manager. But we can't survive without it, we all depend on it for our living.'

So a few peasants, in the name of the village commune, begged the lady not to sell any of her land to the innkeeper and to let them buy it, offering her a better price. The lady agreed. Then the members of the commune thought of

buying the whole estate. They met once, they met twice, but no progress was made: the Devil had set them at loggerheads and there was nothing they could agree upon. In the end they decided to buy the land in separate lots, each according to what he could afford. The lady agreed to this as well.

One day Pakhom learned that one of his neighbours was buying about fifty acres and that the lady had taken half payment in cash, allowing the man one year to pay the balance. This made Pakhom very envious. 'They'll buy up all the land,' he thought, 'and I'll be left with nothing.' So he conferred with his wife.

'Everyone's buying land,' he said. 'We must get hold of twenty acres, or thereabouts. If we don't we won't be able to live, what with that manager bleeding us white with fines.'

So they racked their brains as to how they could buy some of the land. They had a hundred roubles saved up, so that by selling a foal and half their bees, by sending one of their sons out to work for someone who paid wages in advance and borrowing from a brother-in-law, they managed to scrape together half the money.

Then Pakhom took the money, chose about thirty acres of partly wooded land and went off to the lady to see if he could strike a deal. He managed to get the thirty acres, they shook hands on it and Pakhom paid a deposit. Then they went into town and signed the deeds, Pakhom paying half cash down and pledging to settle the balance within two years.

And so Pakhom now had land. He borrowed money for seeds and sowed the newly bought land; the harvest was excellent. Within a year he had repaid both the lady and his brother-in-law. Now he was a landowner, in the full sense of

the word: he ploughed and sowed his own fields, reaped his own hay, cut his own timber and could pasture his cattle on his own land. Whenever he rode out to plough the land which was now his for ever, or to inspect his young corn and meadows, he was filled with joy. He felt that the grass that grew and the flowers that bloomed were different from any other grass and flowers. Before, when he had ridden over that land, it had seemed the same as any other. But now it was something quite special.

3

So Pakhom lived a landowner's life and he was happy. And in fact all would have been well had other peasants not trespassed on his cornfields and meadows. He spoke to them very politely, but they took no notice. Herdsmen let their cows stray on to his meadows, then horses wandered into his corn on their way home from night pasture. Again and again Pakhom drove them out without taking further action, but in the end he lost patience and complained to the District Court. He knew very well that the peasants weren't doing it deliberately but because they were short of land. But still he thought, 'I can't let this go on. Before long they'll have destroyed all I have. I must teach them a lesson.'

So he taught them a lesson in court, then another, making several of them pay fines. Pakhom's neighbours resented this and once again began to let their cattle stray on his land, this time on purpose. One night someone managed to get into Pakhom's wood and felled about ten young lime-trees

for their bark. Next day, when Pakhom was riding through his wood, he suddenly noticed something white on the ground. He went nearer and saw tree-trunks lying all around, stripped of their bark, with the stumps lying nearby. 'If he'd only just cut one or two down, but that devil's left me with one tree standing and cleared the rest.' Pakhom seethed with anger. 'Oh, if I knew who did it I'd show him a thing or two!' For a long time he racked his brains and finally concluded, 'It must be Semyon, it can't be anyone else.' So off he went to search Semyon's place, but he found nothing and all the two men did was swear at each other. Pakhom was more convinced than ever that it was Semyon's work and he lodged a complaint. The magistrates sat for ages debating the case and finally acquitted Semyon for lack of evidence. This incensed Pakhom even more and he had a stormy session with the village elder and the magistrates.

'You are hand in glove with thieves,' he protested. 'If you were honest men you wouldn't let a thief like him off the hook.'

As a result Pakhom fell out with the magistrates as well as his neighbours, who threatened to burn his cottage down.

And so, although Pakhom had plenty of leg-room now, he felt that the commune was hemming him in.

Around that time rumours were in the air that many peasants were leaving to settle in new parts of the country. Pakhom thought, '*I* don't really need to go away, what with all that land of mine. But if some of the villagers were to go there'd be more room for others. I could buy their land and make my estate bigger. Life would be easier then, but as things are, it's still too cramped here for my liking.'

One day a peasant who was passing through stopped at Pakhom's cottage. They let him stay the night and gave him food. Pakhom asked where he was from and the man replied that he had come from the south, from the other side of the Volga, where he had been working. Then he told how people from his own village had settled there, joined the commune and had been allotted twenty-five acres each. 'The land is so fertile,' he said, 'that rye grows as high as a horse and it's so thick you can make a whole sheaf from only five handfuls! One peasant arrived with a copeck and only his bare hands to work with and now he has six horses and two cows.'

Pakhom was terribly excited by this news. 'Why should I have to scrape a living cooped up here,' he thought, 'when I could be leading a good life somewhere else? I could sell the land and cottage and with the money I'd be able to build myself a house there and start a whole new farm. But here there's no room to breathe and I get nothing but aggravation. I must go and find out what it's like for myself.'

When summer came he was ready and he set off. He went down the Volga to Samara by steamboat, then walked the remaining three hundred miles to the new settlement, which was just as the visitor had described. All the men had plenty of space, each having been allotted twenty-five acres without charge and welcomed into the commune. Anyone who had the money could also buy as much of the finest freehold land as he wanted, at three roubles an acre – there was no limit!

Towards autumn, after finding out all he needed to know, Pakhom went home and started selling up. He sold the land at a profit, his home and all his cattle, resigned from the

commune and waited until the spring, when he left with his family for the new settlement.

4

When he arrived with his family Pakhom managed to get himself on the register of a large village commune, having duly moistened the elders' throats. All was signed and sealed and Pakhom was granted a hundred acres (twenty for each member of his family, in different fields), besides the use of the communal pasture. Then he put up some buildings and stocked his farm with cattle. The allotted land alone was three times as much as at home and it was perfect for growing corn. He was ten times better off here, for he had plenty of arable land and pasturage, and he was able to keep as many cattle as he wanted.

At first, while he was busy building and stocking up, everything seemed wonderful. But no sooner had he settled down to his new life than he began to feel cramped even here. During the first year he had sowed wheat on the allotted land and the crop had been excellent. But when he wanted to sow more wheat he found he needed more land: the other land he had been allotted was not suitable for wheat. In the south wheat is sown only on grass or on fallow land. They sow it for one or two years and then leave it fallow until the land is overgrown with feather-grass again. This type of land was in great demand and there wasn't enough to go round, so that people quarrelled over it. The richer ones sowed their own, whilst the poorer ones had to mortgage

theirs to merchants to pay their taxes. Pakhom wanted to sow more wheat, so the following year he rented some fields from a dealer for one year. He sowed a great deal of wheat and had a good crop. But the fields were a long way from the village and the wheat had to be carted more than ten miles. Then Pakhom noticed that some peasant farmers with large homesteads in the neighbourhood were becoming very wealthy. 'What if I bought some freehold land and built myself a homestead like theirs?' he wondered. 'Then everything would be within easy reach.' And he tried to think how he could buy some.

Pakhom farmed the same way for three years, renting land and sowing wheat. They were good years, the crops were good and he was able to save some money. But Pakhom grew tired of having to rent land, year after year, of having to waste his time scrambling after it. Whenever good land came up for sale the peasants would immediately fall over themselves to buy it and it would all be gone before he could do anything: he was never quick enough and so he had no land for sowing his wheat. So in the third year he went halves with a merchant in buying a plot of pasture land outright from some peasants. They had already ploughed it when someone sued the peasants over it and as a result all their work was wasted. 'If it had been *my* land,' Pakhom thought, 'I wouldn't have been under an obligation to anyone and I wouldn't have got into that mess.'

So Pakhom tried to discover where to buy some freehold land. He came across a peasant who, having purchased some thirteen hundred acres, had then gone bankrupt and was selling the land off very cheaply. Pakhom bargained with

him. After much haggling they finally agreed upon fifteen hundred roubles, half cash down, half to be paid at a later date. The deal was all but signed and sealed when a passing merchant called at Pakhom's to have his horses fed. They drank tea together and got into conversation. The merchant said that he was on his way back from the far-off land of the Bashkirs, where he had bought some thirteen thousand acres for a mere thousand roubles. When Pakhom questioned him further the merchant told him, 'All I had to do was give the old men there a few presents – a hundred roubles' worth of silk robes and carpets, a chest of tea, and vodka for anyone who wanted it. I managed to get the land for twenty copecks an acre.' He showed Pakhom the title deeds. 'The land is near a river and it's all beautiful grassy steppe.'

Pakhom continued to ply him with questions.

'There's so much land that you couldn't walk round it all in a year. It all belongs to the Bashkirs. Yes, the people there are as stupid as sheep and you can get land off them for practically nothing.'

'Well,' Pakhom thought, 'why should I pay a thousand roubles for thirteen hundred acres and saddle myself with debt? To think what I could buy with the same money down there!'

5

Pakhom asked him how to get there and as soon as he had said goodbye to the merchant he prepared to leave. He left his wife behind and set off, taking a workman with him. First they stopped off in town and bought a chest of tea, vodka

and other presents, just as the old merchant had advised. Then they travelled for miles and miles until, on the seventh day, they reached the Bashkir settlement. Everything was as the merchant had described: the people lived on the steppe, near a river, in tents of thick felt. They neither ploughed the soil nor ate bread, and their cattle and horses wandered in herds over the steppe. The foals were tethered behind the tents and the mares brought over to them twice a day. These mares were milked and from the milk kumiss was made. The women also made cheese from the kumiss and all the men seemed concerned with was drinking kumiss and tea, eating mutton and playing their pipes. All of them were cheerful and well-fed, and they spent the whole summer idling about. The Bashkirs were very ignorant, knew no Russian, but were kindly people.

The moment they spotted Pakhom, the Bashkirs streamed out of their tents and surrounded their visitor. An interpreter was found and Pakhom told him that he had come about some land. The Bashkirs were delighted and took Pakhom off to one of the finest tents, where they made him sit on some rugs piled with cushions, while they formed a circle and offered him tea and kumiss. Then they slaughtered a sheep and fed him with mutton. Pakhom fetched the presents from his cart, handed them round and shared the tea out. The Bashkirs were delighted. For a while they talked away amongst themselves and then told the interpreter to translate.

'They want me to tell you,' the interpreter said, 'that they've taken a great liking to you and that it's our custom to do all we can to please a guest and repay him for his gifts. You have given us presents, so please tell us if there is

anything of ours that you would like so we can show our gratitude.'

'What I like most of all here,' Pakhom replied, 'is your land. Back home there isn't enough to go round and, what's more, the soil is exhausted. But here you have plenty and it looks very good. I've never seen soil like it.'

The interpreter translated and then the Bashkirs went into a lengthy conference. Although Pakhom did not understand, he could see how cheerful they were, laughing and shouting. Then they all became quiet, glanced at Pakhom and the interpreter continued, 'I'm to tell you that they would be only too pleased to let you have as much land as you like in return for your kindness. All you have to do is point it out and it will be yours.'

Then they conferred again and started arguing about something. Pakhom asked what it was and the interpreter told him, 'Some of them are saying they should first consult the elder about the land. They can't do anything without his permission, but some of the others say it's not necessary.'

6

While the Bashkirs were arguing, a man in a fox-fur cap suddenly came into the tent, whereupon they all became quiet and stood up.

'It's the elder,' the interpreter explained.

Pakhom immediately fetched his best robe and presented it with five pounds of tea to the elder, who accepted the gifts and then sat in the place of honour. The Bashkirs immedi-

ately started telling him something. After listening for a while the elder motioned with his head for them to be quiet and then spoke to Pakhom in Russian.

'Well now,' he said. 'It's all right. Choose whatever land you like, there's plenty of it.'

'How can I just go and take whatever I like?' Pakhom wondered. 'I must have it all signed and sealed somehow. Now they tell me it's mine, but who knows, they might change their minds?' So he told them, 'Thank you for your kind words. Yes, you do have a great deal of land, but I need only a little. However, I would like to be sure which will be mine, so couldn't it be measured and made over to me by some sort of contract? Our lives are in God's hands and although you good people are willing to give me the land now, it's possible your children might want it back again.'

'What you say is true,' said the elder. 'We can have a contract drawn up.'

Pakhom said, 'I've heard that you made some land over to a merchant not long ago, together with the title deeds. I would like you to do the same with me.'

The elder understood. 'That's no problem,' he said. 'We have a clerk here and we can ride into town and have the documents properly witnessed and signed.'

'But what about the price?' Pakhom asked.

'We have a set price – a thousand roubles a day.'

Pakhom did not understand.

'What kind of rate is that – a *day*? How many acres would that be?'

'We don't reckon your way. We sell by the day. However

much you can walk round in one day will be yours. And the price is a thousand roubles a day.'

Pakhom was amazed. 'Well, a man can walk round a lot of land in one day,' he said.

The elder burst out laughing. 'Well, all of it will be yours,' he replied. 'But there's one condition: if you don't return to your starting-point the same day, your money will be forfeited.'

'But how can I mark where I've been?'

'We'll all go to whatever place you select and wait until you've completed your circuit. You must take a spade, dig a hole at every turning and leave the turf piled up. Afterwards, we will go from hole to hole with a plough. You may make as large a circuit as you like, only you must be back at your starting-point by sunset. All the land you can walk round will be yours.'

Pakhom was absolutely delighted. An early start was decided on and after talking for a while they drank kumiss, ate some mutton and then had tea. This went on until nightfall. Then the Bashkirs made up a feather-bed for Pakhom and left. They promised to be ready to ride out to the chosen spot before sunrise.

7

Pakhom lay down on the feather-bed, but the thought of all that land kept him awake. 'Tomorrow,' he thought, 'I shall mark out a really large stretch. In one day I can easily walk thirty-five miles. The days are long now – just think how

much land I'll have from walking that distance! I'll sell the poorer bits, or let it to the peasants. I'll take the best for myself and farm it. I'll have two ox-ploughs and hire a couple of labourers to work them. Yes, I'll cultivate about a hundred and fifty acres and let the cattle graze the rest.'

Pakhom did not sleep a wink that night and dozed off only just before dawn. The moment he fell asleep he had a dream: he seemed to be lying in the same tent and could hear someone roaring with laughter outside. Wondering who was laughing like that he got up, went out and saw that same Bashkir elder sitting there, holding his sides and rolling about in fits of laughter. He went closer and asked, 'What are you laughing at?' And then he saw that it wasn't the elder at all, but the merchant who had called on him a few days before and told him about the land. And just as Pakhom asked him, 'Have you been here long?' the merchant turned into the peasant who had come up from the Volga and visited him at home. And then Pakhom saw that it wasn't the peasant, but the Devil himself, with horns and hoofs, sitting there laughing his head off, while before him lay a barefoot man wearing only shirt and trousers. When Pakhom took a closer look he saw that the man was dead and that it was himself. Pakhom woke up in a cold sweat. 'The things one dreams about!' he thought. Then he looked round and saw that it was getting light at the open door – dawn was breaking. 'I must go and wake them,' he thought, 'it's time to start.' So Pakhom got up, roused the workman, who was sleeping in the cart, ordered him to harness the horse and went off to wake the Bashkirs. 'It's time to go out on the steppe and measure the land,' he said. The Bashkirs got up, assembled,

and then the elder came and joined them. They drank some more kumiss and offered Pakhom tea, but he was impatient to be off. 'If we're going,' he said, 'let's go. It's time.'

8

So the Bashkirs got ready and left, some on horses, others in carts. Pakhom went to his little cart with him. They came out on to the open steppe just as the sun was rising. They climbed a small hill (called a 'shikhan' in Bashkir). Then the Bashkirs got out of their carts, dismounted from their horses and gathered in one place. The elder went over to Pakhom and pointed.

'Look,' he said, 'that's all ours, as far as the eye can see. Choose any part you like.'

Pakhom's eyes lit up, for the land was all virgin soil, flat as the palm of one's hand, black as poppy-seed, with different kinds of grass growing breast-high in the hollows.

The elder took off his fox-fur cap and put it on the ground.

'Let this be the marker: this is the starting point to which you must return. All the land you can walk round will be yours.'

Pakhom took out his money, placed it on the cap, took off his outer coat, so that he was wearing only a sleeveless undercoat, tightened his belt below the waist and stuffed a small bag of bread inside his shirt. Then he tied a flask of water to the belt, pulled up his boots, took the spade from his workman and was ready to leave. He could not decide which

direction to take at first as the land was so good everywhere. Then he decided, 'It's all good land, so I'll walk towards the sunrise.' He turned to the east, stretching himself as he waited for the sun to appear above the horizon. 'There's no point in wasting time,' he thought. 'And it's easier walking while it's still cool.' The moment the sun's rays came flooding over the horizon Pakhom put the spade on one shoulder and walked out on to the steppe.

Pakhom walked neither quickly nor slowly. When he had gone about three quarters of a mile he stopped, dug a hole and piled the pieces of turf high on top of each other so that they were easily visible. The stiffness had now gone from his legs and he lengthened his stride. A little further on he stopped again and dug another hole.

When Pakhom looked back he could see quite clearly the small hill tyres of the cart-wheels. Pakhom guessed that he had covered about three miles. He was beginning to feel warmer, so he tool off his undercoat, flung it over his shoulder and walked another three miles. It was hot, and a look at the sun reminded him it was time for breakfast.

'Well, that's the first stretch completed!' he thought. 'But there are four to a day and it's too early to start turning. I must take these boots off, though.'

So he sat down, took off his boots, stuck them behind his belt and moved on. The going was easy now and he thought. 'I'll do another three miles and then turn left. The land's so beautiful here, it would be a pity to miss out on any of it. The further I go, the better the land gets.' So for a while he carried straight on and when he looked back the hill was

barely visible and the people on it looked like black ants; he could just glimpse something that glinted in the sun.

'Well,' thought Pakhom, 'I've walked enough in this direction, I should be turning now. Besides, I'm stewing in this heat and terribly thirsty.' So he stopped, dug a large hole, piled up the turf, untied his flask, drank and then turned sharp left. On and on he walked – the grass was higher here and it was very hot.

Pakhom began to feel tired. He glanced at the sun and saw that it was noon. 'Well,' he thought, 'I must have a little rest.' So he stopped, sat down and had some bread and water. He did not stretch out, though, thinking, 'Once I lie down I'll fall asleep.' After a few minutes he carried on. At first it was easy – the food had given him strength. But by now it was extremely hot and he began to feel sleepy. Still, he kept going and thought of the proverb, 'A moment's pain can be a lifetime's gain.'

He had walked a long way in the same direction and was just about to turn left when he spotted a lush hollow and decided it would be a pity to lose it. 'What a good place for growing flax!' he thought. So he carried straight on until he had walked right round the low-lying meadows, dug a hole the other side, and then he turned the second corner. Pakhom looked back at the hill: it was shimmering in the heat and through the haze it was difficult to see all the people there – they were at least ten miles away. 'Well,' thought Pakhom, 'I've made those sides too long, this one has to be shorter.' So he started the third side, quickening his step. He looked at the sun and saw that it was already half way to the horizon, but he had completed only about

one mile of the third side. The starting-point was still ten miles away. 'No,' he thought, 'although it will make the land a bit lopsided I must take the shortest way back. It's no good trying to grab too much, I've quite enough already!'

Pakhom hastily dug another hole and headed straight for the hill.

9

On the way back Pakhom found the going tough. The heat had exhausted him, his bare feet were cut and bruised and his legs were giving way. He wanted to rest, but this was out of the question – he would never get back by sunset. The sun waits for no man and was sinking lower and lower. 'Oh,' he wondered, 'have I blundered, trying to take too much? What if I'm not back in time?' He looked towards the hill, then at the sun. The hill was far off, the sun was close to the horizon.

But Pakhom struggled on. Although it was very hard, he walked faster and faster. On and on he went – but there was still a long way to go. He started running and threw away his coat, boots, flask, cap, keeping only the spade which he used for leaning on. 'Oh dear,' he thought, 'I've been too greedy. Now I've ruined it. I'll never get back by sunset.' His fear made him only more breathless. On he ran, his shirt soaking and his trousers clinging to him: his throat was parched. His lungs were working like a blacksmith's bellows, his heart beat like a hammer and his legs did not seem to be his – he felt that they were breaking . . . Pakhom was terrified and thought, 'All this strain will be the death of me.'

Although he feared death, he could not stop. 'If I stopped now, after coming all this way – well, they'd call me an idiot!' So on he ran until he was close enough to hear the Bashkirs yelling and cheering him on. Their shouts spurred him on all the more, so he summoned his last ounce of strength and kept running. But by now the sun was almost touching the horizon: veiled in mist, it was large and blood-red. It was about to set, but although it did not have very far to sink it was no distance to the starting-point either. Pakhom could see the people on the hill now, waving their arms and urging him on. He could see the fox-fur cap on the ground with the money on it; he could see the elder sitting there with his arms pressed to his sides. And Pakhom remembered his dream. 'I've plenty of land now, but will God let me live to enjoy it? No, I'm finished . . . I'll never make it.'

Pakhom looked at the sun – it had reached the earth now: half of its great disc had dipped below the horizon. With all the strength he had left Pakhom lurched forwards with his full weight, hardly able to move his legs quickly enough to stop himself falling. He reached the hill – and everything suddenly became dark. He looked round and saw that the sun had set. Pakhom groaned. 'All that effort has been in vain,' he thought. He wanted to stop, when he heard the Bashkirs still cheering him on and he realized that from where he was at the bottom of the hill the sun had apparently set, but not for those on top. Pakhom took a deep breath and rushed up the hill which was still bathed in sunlight. When he reached the top he saw his cap with the elder sitting by it, holding his sides and laughing his head off. Then he remembered the dream and he groaned. His legs gave

way, he fell forward and managed to reach the cap with his hands.

'Oh, well done!' exclaimed the elder. 'That's a lot of land you've earned yourself!'

Pakhom's workman ran up and tried to lift his master, but the blood flowed from his mouth. Pakhom was dead.

The Bashkirs clicked their tongues sympathetically.

Pakhom's workman picked up the spade, dug a grave for his master – six feet from head to heel, which was exactly the right length – and buried him.

What Men Live By

We know that we have passed from death unto life, because we love the brethren. He that loveth not his brother abideth in death. (I John iii, 14)

But whoso hath this world's good, and seeth his brother have need, and shutteth up his bowels of compassion from him, how dwelleth the love of God in him? (I John iii, 17)

My little children, let us not love in word, neither in tongue: but in deed and in truth. (I John iii, 18)

. . . for love is of God; and every one that loveth is born of God, and knoweth God. (I John iv, 7)

He that loveth not knoweth not God; for God is love. (I John iv, 8)

No man hath seen God at any time. If we love one another, God dwelleth in us . . . (I John iv, 12)

God is love; and he that dwelleth in love dwelleth in God, and God in him. (I John iv, 16)

If a man say, I love God, and hateth his brother, he is a liar: for he that loveth not his brother whom he hath seen, how can he love God whom he hath not seen? (I John iv, 20)

1

Once there was a shoemaker who had neither house nor land of his own and who lived in a peasant's cottage with his wife and children, supporting them by what work he could get. Bread was expensive but his work was cheap and the little he earned was spent on food for his family. He and his wife had only one winter coat between them and even that was in a sorry state. For the past two years he had been saving to buy sheepskins for a new one.

By autumn he had scraped together a small sum: there was the three-rouble note that his wife kept in a little wooden box, as well as the five roubles and twenty copecks that some of the villagers owed him.

One morning he decided to go to the village to buy the skins. He put his wife's wadded twill jacket over his shirt and over that his own cloth coat. After breakfast he put the three-rouble note in his pocket, cut himself a walking-stick and set off.

'With the five roubles that one of them owes me,' he thought, 'plus the three I already have, I should have enough to buy the sheepskins.'

When he reached the village he stopped at a cottage, but the owner was out. His wife did not have the money, but she promised to send her husband over with it by the end of the week. So he called on another peasant who swore he was short of cash and that all he could manage was twenty copecks that were owing for some boot repairs. And then,

when the shoemaker tried to buy the skins on credit, the dealer would not trust him.

'Bring me the money first,' he said. 'Then you can pick whatever skins you like. We all know how hard it is to collect what's owing to us!'

And so the shoemaker did no business that day, apart from twenty copecks for the repairs and a pair of felt boots that needed soling.

All this depressed the shoemaker and after spending the twenty copecks on vodka he set off for home without any skins. Earlier that morning he had felt a sharp nip in the air, but after a few vodkas he warmed up – even though he had no proper winter coat. As he walked down the road, striking frozen clods of earth with his stick in one hand and swinging the felt boots in the other, he started talking to himself.

'I feel quite warm without a coat,' he said. 'I've only had a drop, yet I can feel it rushing through every vein in my body. I don't need any sheepskins! I'm going home, with all my troubles behind me. That's the sort of man I am! Why should I worry? I can survive without a new coat – I won't need one for ages. Only, the wife won't be too happy. But it's really rotten when you do a job and the customer tries to string you along and doesn't pay up. You just wait – if you don't bring me the money I'll have the shirt off your back, I swear it! It's a bit much, what with a measly twenty copecks at a time. What can I do with twenty copecks? Spend it on drink, that's all. You say you're hard up. Well, what about me? You've a house, cattle, everything, but all I

have is on my back. You grow your own corn, while I have to go out and buy mine. Whatever happens I must spend three roubles a week on bread alone. By the time I get home there won't be any left and I'll have to fork out another rouble and a half. So, you'd better pay up!'

The shoemaker kept rambling on like this until he drew near the wayside chapel at the bend in the road where something whitish just behind it caught his eye. But by now it was growing dark and although he strained his eyes he could not make out what it was. 'There wasn't any stone there before,' he thought. 'Perhaps it's a cow? No, it doesn't look like one at all. From the head it looks like a man and it's all white. But what would a man be doing there?'

He went a few steps closer and could now make it out quite clearly. How amazing! It *was* a man sitting there, but he could not see if he were dead or alive, and he was naked and quite motionless, his back propped against the chapel wall. The shoemaker was terrified and thought, 'A man's been murdered, stripped naked and dumped. If I go any nearer I might get mixed up in all sorts of troubles.'

And so the shoemaker went on his way. He walked behind the chapel to avoid having to look at him again. After a short distance he turned round and saw that the man was no longer leaning against the wall, but was moving, as if trying to see who he was. The shoemaker felt even more frightened and thought, 'Shall I go back or simply carry on? If I go back something terrible might happen. Who knows what kind of man he might be? I bet he's up to no good. Besides, he might suddenly jump to his feet and start choking the life out of me – and there'd be nothing I could do about it. And

if he doesn't throttle me I might get lumbered with looking after him. But how can I help a naked man? I couldn't let him have the last shirt off my back. Please God, help me!'

And the shoemaker quickened his stride. He had almost left the chapel behind when his conscience began to prick him. He stopped in the middle of the road.

'How could you do such a thing, Semyon?' he reproached himself. 'That man might be dying miserably and you're such a coward you'd leave him there to die. Or have you become so rich all of a sudden that you're scared stiff he might steal all your money? You should be ashamed, Semyon!'

And he turned round again and went right up to the man.

2

After a close look Semyon could see that he was young and healthy. There were no bruises on his body: he was just chilled to the bone and terrified. There he sat, leaning forward without looking at Semyon and apparently too weak to raise his eyes. When Semyon was right next to him he suddenly seemed to wake as if from a trance. He turned his head, opened his eyes and looked straight at Semyon. That one look was enough to allay all Semyon's fears. He threw down the felt boots, undid his belt, laid it over the boots and took off his cloth coat.

'There's no time for talking,' he said. 'Put that on – and be quick about it!'

Then Semyon took the man under the arms and tried to lift him, but he got to his feet without any help. And then

Semyon saw that his body was slender and clean, that his legs and arms bore no trace of any wounds; his face was mild and gentle. Semyon threw his coat over his shoulders, but the man could not find the sleeves, so Semyon guided his arms into them, pulled on the coat, wrapped it around him and fastened it with his belt.

Then Semyon took off his tattered cap, intending to put it on the naked man's head, but he felt the cold on his own head and thought, 'I'm completely bald, while he's got long, curly hair.' And he put it back on again. 'It would be better to give him the boots,' he thought.

So he made the man sit down again and put the felt boots on his feet, after which he said, 'There you are, my friend. Stretch your legs a bit and warm yourself. Don't worry, it will all be sorted out later. Now, can you walk?'

The man stood up, looked tenderly at Semyon, but was unable to say one word.

'Why don't you say something? Come on, we can't spend all winter here, we must be on our way. Here, you can lean on my stick if you feel weak. Right, come on!'

And the man started walking – and he walked effortlessly, without lagging behind.

As they went down the road Semyon asked, 'Where are you from?'

'Not from these parts.'

'I thought so – I know everyone round here. But how did you come to be there, by the chapel?'

'I cannot tell you that.'

'Did some men attack you?'

'No, no one harmed me. It was God who punished me.'

'Well, we are all in His hands. All the same, you must have somewhere to go. Where are you heading?'

'Nowhere in particular.'

Semyon was amazed. The man did not strike him as a ruffian, he was so softly spoken, yet he revealed nothing about himself. 'Anything can happen in this world,' Semyon reflected and he told the man, 'All right, come home with me, even if it is a bit out of your way.'

As Semyon walked down the road the stranger did not lag behind for one moment, but kept abreast. The wind got up and the cold air crept under Semyon's shirt. The drink was beginning to wear off and he felt chilled to the marrow.

Sniffling as he went, he wrapped his wife's jacket tighter around himself and thought, 'So much for sheepskins! I go off to buy some and all I do is come home without even the old coat on my back, and with a naked stranger into the bargain! Matryona won't be too pleased about that!' And the thought of his wife depressed him. But the moment he looked at the stranger he remembered the look he had given him at the chapel and his heart filled with joy.

3

Semyon's wife had finished her chores early that day. She had chopped the wood, fetched water, fed the children, had a bite to eat herself and had then sat for a long time wondering when she should bake the bread – that same day or the next. There was still one thick slice left.

'If Semyon has his dinner in the village,' she thought, 'then he won't want much for supper and there'll be enough bread for tomorrow.'

She turned the slice over, 'I shan't do any baking today,' she decided, 'there's only enough flour for one loaf. But we can make this last till Friday.'

So Matryona put the bread away and sat down at the table to patch her husband's shirt. As she worked she thought of him buying the sheepskins for the new winter coat.

'I hope the dealer won't swindle him. He's so simple, that husband of mine. He'd never cheat a soul himself and even a little child could trick him. Eight roubles is a lot of money, enough to buy very good sheepskins. Not the best quality tanned ones perhaps, but still good enough for a nice coat. Last winter was so hard without a proper one! I couldn't even go down to the river, couldn't go anywhere. And when he left this morning he took all the warm clothes we have, leaving me with nothing to wear. Now, he didn't leave all that early. All the same, it's time he was back. I hope my old man hasn't gone drinking!'

These thoughts had just crossed Matryona's mind when the front steps creaked and someone came in. Matryona stuck her needle into the shirt and went out into the hall. There she saw two men – Semyon and someone in felt boots and without a cap.

Matryona immediately smelt the vodka on her husband's breath. 'So, I was right, he's been on the drink,' she thought. And when she saw him standing there, empty-handed and with a guilty grin on his face, wearing nothing but the jacket

she had lent him, her heart sank. 'He's gone and spent all that money drinking with some good-for-nothing. What's more, he's got the nerve to bring him home.'

Matryona ushered them in and followed them into the living-room. Now she could see that the stranger was a thin young man and that he was wearing her husband's coat. She could see no shirt under it and he had no cap. Once inside he stood quite still and kept looking down. Matryona concluded that he was a bad lot, as he seemed so nervous.

Frowning, she went over to the stove and waited to see what they would do next.

Semyon took off his cap and sat down on the bench as if he had done no wrong.

'Come on, Matryona, let's have some supper!' he said.

Matryona muttered something to herself and stayed quite still by the stove. She kept looking first at one, then the other, shaking her head. Semyon realized that his wife was annoyed, but there was nothing he could do about it. Pretending not to notice, he took the stranger by the arm.

'Sit down,' he said. 'Let's have something to eat.'

The stranger sat on the bench.

'Well, don't you have anything?'

Matryona lost her temper. 'Yes, I do, but not for you. It seems you've drunk your brains away. You went out to buy some sheepskins and back you come without even the coat you left in. What's more, you bring some half-naked tramp back with you. I don't have any supper for a pair of drunkards like you!'

'Now that's enough of your stupid tongue-wagging, Matryona! You might at least ask who he is.'

'And you can tell me what you did with the money.'

Semyon felt in his pocket, took out the three-rouble note and unfolded it.

'Here it is. Trifonov wouldn't give me any money, but he promised to pay up in a day or so.'

Matryona grew even more furious: in addition to not buying the sheepskins, her husband had lent their only coat to some naked stranger. What's more, he'd brought him back home.

She snatched the note from the table and went off to hide it somewhere.

'I've no supper for you,' she told them. 'You can't expect me to feed every naked drunkard.'

'And you mind your tongue, Matryona. First hear what he has to say . . .'

'What sense will I get from a drunken fool like him? I was right in not wanting to marry an old soak like you! You sold all Mother's linen for drink. And then, instead of buying sheepskins you spend the money on drink.'

Semyon tried hard to make his wife understand that all he had spent on drink was a mere twenty copecks and to explain where he had found the stranger. But she would not let him get a word in edgeways, rattling away nineteen to the dozen and even reminding him of things that had happened ten years ago. On and on she went, until finally she dashed over to Semyon and grabbed his sleeve.

'Give me my jacket back, it's the only one I have and you took it to wear yourself. Give it back, you flea-bitten dog. May you die of a fit!'

Semyon began taking the jacket off and turned a sleeve

inside-out, but his wife tugged so hard that it came apart at the seams. Then she seized it, threw it over her head and made for the door. But then she stopped. Her heart seemed to melt and she felt that she wanted to banish all those spiteful feelings and to find out who that man really was.

4

As she stood there, quite still, Matryona said, 'If he were an honest man he wouldn't be going around without a shirt to his back. And if you'd been doing what you were supposed to you'd have told me where you picked up this fine young fellow!'

'All right, I'll tell you. I was on my way home when I saw this man sitting by the chapel, naked and frozen. Now, it's not the kind of weather to go about naked! God must have led me to him, or he'd have perished. What could I do? Who knows what may have happened to him? So, I made him stand up, clothed him and brought him back here. Please don't be angry, Matryona, it's sinful. Don't forget that we must all die one day.'

Matryona was about to give him a piece of her mind again, but then she looked at the stranger and became silent. There he sat, motionless, on the edge of the bench, his hands folded on his knees, his head drooping on his breast. His eyes were closed and he wrinkled his face as if something were choking him. Matryona still said nothing, but Semyon asked, 'Matryona, is there no love of God within you?'

At these words Matryona glanced at the stranger and her heart suddenly filled with pity. She came back from the door, went over to the stove, took out the supper, placed a cup on the table, poured out some kvass, brought out the last slice of bread and set out a knife and some spoons. Please eat,' she said.

Semyon nudged the stranger and told him, 'Come and sit at the table.'

Semyon divided the bread into small pieces and they started eating. Matryona sat at one corner of the table, her head on her hand, gazing at the stranger. And she was filled with pity and her heart went out to him. Suddenly, his face brightened, the wrinkles disappeared and he looked up at Matryona and smiled.

After supper Matryona cleared the table and began questioning him.

'Where are you from?'

'Not from these parts.'

'How did you come to be by the wayside?'

'I cannot tell you.'

'Who stole your clothes?'

'God punished me.'

'And you were lying there, all naked?'

'Yes, naked and freezing. And then Semyon saw me and took pity on me. He took off his coat, put it over me and insisted I came home with him. You have given me food and drink and shown compassion. God will reward you!'

Matryona got up, took from the window-sill the old shirt of Semyon's she had been patching and handed it to the stranger. Then she found him some trousers.

'Here, I see you've no shirt, so put this on and lie down where you like – up on the sleeping-bench or over the stove.'

The stranger took off the coat, put on the shirt and trousers and lay on the sleeping-bench. Matryona blew out the candle, took the coat and joined her husband over the stove.

Matryona drew the skirts of the coat over herself and lay down. But she did not fall asleep, for she could not get that stranger out of her mind.

When she remembered that he had eaten their last slice of bread and that they would have none for tomorrow, and that she had given him the shirt and trousers, she became terribly dejected. But then, when she recalled his smile her heart leapt up. For a long time she lay awake and she noticed that Semyon was awake too, as he kept pulling the coat up.

'Semyon!'

'What is it?'

'You two have eaten the last slice of bread and I haven't prepared any more. I don't know what we're going to do tomorrow. Perhaps I can borrow some from our neighbour Malanya.'

'Yes, we'll get by, we won't starve.'

Matryona lay silently for a while and then she said, 'He seems to be a good man, only he doesn't tell us anything about himself.'

'I suppose he can't.'

'Semyon!'

'What?'

'We're always giving, but why does nobody ever give *us* anything?'

Semyon didn't know what to reply. All he said was, 'Let's

talk about that another time,' after which he turned over and went to sleep.

5

Next morning, when Semyon woke up, the children were still asleep and his wife had gone over to the neighbour's to borrow some bread. Only the stranger was sitting on the bench, wearing the old trousers and shirt and looking up. His face was brighter than the evening before. Semyon said, 'Well, my friend. The belly needs food and the body clothes. We all have to earn a living, so what sort of work can you do?'

'I can't do anything.'

Semyon was amazed and replied, 'If a man has the will he can learn anything.'

'Yes, men work for their living, so I'll work too.'

'What's your name?'

'Mikhail.'

'Well, Mikhail, if you don't want to tell us about yourself that's your affair. But we have to earn our living. If you do as I tell you I'll see you have enough to eat.'

'God bless you! I'll learn how to work, just tell me what to do.'

Semyon took a piece of yarn, wound it round his fingers and twisted it.

'It's not hard, just watch . . .'

Mikhail watched and right away he caught the knack, winding the yarn and twisting it just like Semyon.

Then Semyon showed him how to wax it and Mikhail understood at once. Then he showed him how to draw it through and how to stitch. Again Mikhail immediately understood.

Whatever Semyon showed him he mastered right away and within three days was working as if he had been making shoes all his life. He would work without any let-up and ate very little. Only when one job was finished would he stop for a moment and silently look up. He never went out, only spoke when he really had to, and he never joked or laughed.

And in fact the only time they had seen him smile was on that very first evening, when Matryona had given him supper.

6

The days passed, weeks passed, and a year ran its course. Mikhail was still living with Semyon and working for him. The word got round that Semyon's new workman could make boots better and stronger than anyone else. People from all over the district came to Semyon for new boots and he prospered.

One winter's day Semyon and Mikhail were sitting at their work when a three-horse carriage on sleigh runners drove up to the cottage, its bells gaily ringing. When they looked out of the window they saw it had stopped right outside. A boy jumped down from the box and opened the carriage door. A gentleman in a fur coat stepped out, walked up to

the front door and climbed the steps. Matryona rushed to fling open the door.

As he came in, the gentleman had to lower his head and then straighten up. But still his head almost touched the ceiling and he filled a whole corner of the room.

Semyon stood up and marvelled at the gentleman: he had never seen anyone like him. Semyon himself was lean, Mikhail was skinny, while Matryona was as thin as a rake. But this visitor seemed like someone from another world: with his full red face and his bull's neck he seemed to be made of cast iron.

He puffed, took off his fur coat, sat on the bench and asked, 'Who is the master bootmaker here?'

Semyon stepped forward and said, 'I am, Your Honour.'

Then the gentleman shouted to his boy, 'Hey, Fedka, bring the leather!'

The boy ran in with a parcel, which the gentleman took and placed on the table.

'Untie it,' he said. The boy untied it.

Then the gentleman pointed at the leather and told Semyon, 'Now, listen to me, bootmaker. Do you see that leather?'

'Yes, I do, Your Honour.'

'Do you know what kind it is?'

Semyon felt it and said, 'It's very good quality.'

'I should say it's good quality! You fool, I bet you've never set eyes on leather like that. It's German and I paid twenty roubles for it.'

Semyon quailed and said, 'Now where would *I* see leather like that?'

'Yes, where indeed! Could you make me a pair of boots out of it?'

'It's possible, Your Honour.'

'I'll give you possible!' the gentleman shouted. 'Now, see you don't forget for whom you're making them and the quality of the leather you'll be using. I want a pair of boots that will last me a year without losing their shape or coming apart at the stitches. If you can do the job, take the leather and cut it up. But if you can't, you'd better tell me here and now. I'm warning you: if the boots split or lose their shape before the year's out I'll have you clapped in prison. But if they keep their shape and don't split for a year I'll pay you ten roubles.'

Semyon was quite afraid and did not know what to reply. He glanced at Mikhail, nudged him with his elbow and whispered, 'Well, shall I take it on?'

Mikhail nodded as if to say, 'Yes, take it on.'

So Semyon followed Mikhail's advice and undertook to make a pair of boots that would not lose their shape or split for a whole year.

Then the gentleman called the boy over to take off his left boot for him and stretched out his leg.

'Take my measurements!'

Semyon sewed together a strip of paper about seventeen inches long, smoothed it out, knelt down, wiped his hands thoroughly on his apron so as not to dirty the gentleman's sock and started measuring. He took the sole and instep measurements. But when he tried to measure the calf he found that the strip of paper was not long enough – the gentleman's calf was as thick as a log.

'Mind you don't make them too tight in the leg,' he said.

Semyon sewed another piece to the strip of paper, while the gentleman sat wriggling his toes in his sock and surveying the people in the room. And then he noticed Mikhail.

'Who's that over there?' he asked.

'He's my master craftsman, he'll be making the boots.'

'Now you watch out,' the gentleman said, 'remember they have to last a whole year.'

When Semyon turned towards Mikhail he saw that he was not even looking at the gentleman, but staring into the corner, as if someone was standing behind him. Mikhail kept staring until suddenly he smiled and his whole face lit up.

'What are you grinning at, idiot?' the gentleman asked. 'You'd better see to it that the boots are ready on time!'

'They'll be ready whenever you want them,' Mikhail replied.

'Good.'

The gentleman put on his boots again, then his fur coat, which he wrapped tightly around him, and went to the door. But he forgot to lower his head and banged it against the lintel. He cursed and rubbed it. Then he climbed into the carriage and drove off.

As soon as he had gone Semyon remarked, 'He's as tough as nails! You couldn't kill him with a mallet. Why, he nearly knocked the lintel out and still he hardly felt a thing!'

'You'd expect him to be strong with the kind of life he leads,' Matryona said. 'Death itself couldn't touch that iron girder!'

7

'Well, we've taken on the work now,' Semyon told Mikhail, 'and I only hope it doesn't land us in trouble. The leather's very expensive and the gentleman's short-tempered, so we'd better not slip up. Your eyes are sharper than mine and your hands are more skilled, so take the measure and start cutting the leather. I'll sew the vamps later.'

Mikhail obediently took the leather, spread it on the table, folded it in two, took a knife and started cutting.

Matryona went over to watch Mikhail working and was amazed to see what he was doing. Naturally she knew all about boot-making and could see that instead of cutting the leather into the normal shape for boots Mikhail was cutting it into round pieces.

Matryona felt she should point it out, but then she thought, 'Maybe I don't understand how a *gentleman's* boots should be made. Maybe Mikhail knows best, so I won't interfere.'

When he had finished cutting Mikhail took some thread and started sewing the pieces together – not with two ends, as he should have done for boots, but with one end, as if for slippers.

Although Matryona was astonished by this as well, she did not interfere and Mikhail carried on sewing until midday.

When Semyon got up and saw that Mikhail had made a pair of slippers from the gentleman's leather he groaned.

'I don't understand,' he thought, 'how Mikhail, who's

been with me for a whole year without making one mistake, should now go and make such a dreadful mess of things. The gentleman ordered welted high boots and he's made slippers without soles and ruined the leather. How can I face the gentleman now? I can't replace leather of that quality.'

And he told Mikhail, 'What on earth have you done, my friend? You've ruined me! The gentleman ordered high boots and just look what you've made!'

And he was just about to give Mikhail a stern lecture when someone knocked hard on the front door with the iron ring. They looked out of the window and saw that someone had ridden up and was tethering his horse. When the door was opened in came the same young boy who had accompanied the gentleman.

'Good afternoon to you!'

'Good afternoon. What can we do for you?'

'The mistress sent me about those boots.'

'What about them?'

'Just this: the master won't be needing them. He's dead.'

'What did you say?'

'He died in the carriage even before we got home. When we reached the house the others came to help him out, but there he lay, slumped like a sack of potatoes. He was already stiff, stone-dead, and we had a real struggle getting him out. So the mistress told me to come back here. "Tell that shoemaker," she said, "that the gentleman who called and ordered some boots and left the leather won't be needing them and that instead he must make a pair of soft corpse-slippers as soon as he can." She told me to wait until they're ready. So here I am.'

Mikhail collected the offcuts from the table and rolled them up. Then he took the soft slippers he had already made, slapped them together, wiped them with his apron and handed them to the boy, who took them.

'Goodbye, masters! Good luck to you!' he said as he left.

8

Another year passed, then another, until Mikhail was in his sixth year with Semyon. He lived just as before, never going out, speaking only when he had to. And all that time he smiled only twice – when the old woman had first given him supper and then when the rich gentleman called. Semyon thought the world of his workman and no longer inquired where he was from. His only fear was that Mikhail might leave him.

One day they were all at home and Matryona was putting iron pots into the oven, while the children were scampering along the benches and looking out of the windows. Semyon was stitching at one window, while Mikhail was heeling a boot at the other.

One of the little boys ran along the bench to Mikhail, leant on his shoulder and looked through the window.

'Look, Uncle Mikhail! There's a lady with two little girls. I think she's coming here. One of the girls is limping.'

When the boy said this, Mikhail put down his work, turned to the window and looked out into the street.

Semyon was amazed: Mikhail had never looked out into the street before, but now he was glued to the window and staring at something. Semyon, too, looked out and saw that

a well-dressed woman with two little girls in fur coats and thick woollen shawls were in fact coming towards the cottage. The girls were so alike it would have been impossible to tell them apart were it not that one had a crippled left leg and walked with a limp.

The woman climbed the steps, fumbled for the latch and opened the door. She let the little girls in first and then followed them.

'Good day, everyone!' she said.

'Welcome! What can we do for you?'

The woman sat at the table while the girls, feeling shy with all those people in the room, snuggled against her knees.

'I'd like some leather shoes for the girls, for the spring,' she said.

'That's no problem. Although we've never made such small ones before we can do them – either welted or lined with linen. This is Mikhail, my master shoemaker.'

Semyon turned to Mikhail and saw that he had stopped working and was sitting there with his eyes fixed on the little girls.

Semyon was quite surprised. True, the girls were very pretty – plump, with black eyes and rosy little cheeks – and wore fine fur coats and shawls. Still, he could not understand why Mikhail should be staring like that, as if he knew them.

Semyon kept wondering and then started discussing the price with the woman. This was finally agreed and Semyon took his measure. The woman lifted the lame girl on to one knee and said, 'Measure her twice and make one shoe for her lame foot and three for the sound one: they take exactly the same size, because they're twins.'

Semyon took the measurements and inquired about the little lame girl.

'What happened? Such a pretty little girl. Was she born like that?'

'No, she was crushed by her mother.'

Just then Matryona joined in. She was wondering who the woman was and whose children they were.

'You're their mother, aren't you?'

'No, dear woman, I'm not their mother, nor am I a relative. They were complete strangers and I adopted them.'

'They're not your own and yet you seem so fond of them!'

'How can I help being fond of them? I breast-fed them both. I did have a child of my own once, but it pleased God to take him. I didn't love him as much as these little girls, though.'

'So whose are they?'

9

And the woman proceeded to tell them the whole story.

'It all started about six years ago, when these little girls lost their father and mother the same week – the father was buried on the Tuesday and the mother died on the Friday. So, for three days they had no father and on the fourth they lost their mother. At that time my husband and I were farm-workers and our yard was right next door. The father was a lone wolf and worked as a woodcutter. One day when they were cutting down some trees they let one fall right on him and it crushed his insides. They had hardly got him back

to the village when his soul went up to heaven and the same week his widow gave birth to twins – these little girls. She was a poor woman, all on her own, with no other women, young or old, to help her. Alone she gave birth and alone she died.

'The next morning I went to see how she was, but the poor thing was already stiff and cold. When she died she'd rolled over on to this little girl and twisted her leg out of shape. Then the villagers came, washed the body and laid it out. Then they made a coffin and buried her. Good folk they were. So the two little girls were left alone in the world, and who was going to look after them? I happened to be the only woman in that village who'd had a baby at the time and I'd been breast-feeding my first-born for about eight weeks. So I took care of the girls for the time being. The men thought hard about what to do with the orphans and in the end they told me, "You'd better look after them for now, Marya, until we manage to sort something out." So I breast-fed the girl who hadn't been harmed, but not the one who'd been crippled, as I didn't expect her to live. And then I thought to myself, "Why should that little angel be left to fade away?" I took pity on her too and started feeding her, so that in the end I was feeding all three of them – my own first-born and these two, at my own breasts! I was young, strong and well-nourished and God gave me so much milk that it filled my breasts to overflowing. Sometimes I'd feed two at a time, with the third waiting, and when one had had its fill, I'd put the third to my breast. But it was God's will that I should nurse these little girls and bury my own child before he was two years old. And God never gave me another one. But

after that I became quite well off. My second husband's working for a corn merchant and we live at the mill. He earns good money and we live well. But as we've no children of our own I'd be terribly lonely without these two little girls. How can I help loving them? They are the apple of my eye!'

The woman pressed the lame girl to her with one hand and wiped the tears from her cheeks with the other.

Matryona sighed. 'There's a lot of truth in the saying "You can live without mother or father, but you can't live without God."'

They chatted together for a while and then the woman got up to leave. Semyon and his wife saw them out and then they looked at Mikhail: he was sitting there, his arms folded on his knees, and he was looking up and smiling.

10

Semyon went over to Mikhail and asked, 'What is it?'

Mikhail rose from the bench, put down his work, took off his apron, bowed to Semyon and Matryona and said, 'Please forgive me, you good people. God has forgiven me, so please forgive me too.'

And the shoemaker and his wife saw a light shining from Mikhail. And Semyon stood up, bowed in turn and said, 'I can see you are no ordinary mortal and I cannot detain you any longer or question you. But please tell me one thing: why were you so miserable when I first found you and brought you home? And why, when my wife gave you supper, did you smile and from that time onwards brighten up?

And why, when that rich gentleman ordered those boots, did you smile again and become even more cheerful? And why, when that woman brought those little girls here just now, did you smile a third time and become the very picture of joy? Please tell me, Mikhail. What is that light coming from you and why did you smile three times?'

'The light is radiating from me,' Mikhail replied, 'because I had been punished, but now God has forgiven me. And I smiled three times because I was commanded to discover three truths and I have discovered them. I discovered the first truth when your wife took pity on me – that is why I smiled for the first time. The second truth I discovered when that rich gentleman ordered the boots – and then I smiled again. And just now, when I saw those two little girls, I discovered the last of the three truths – and I smiled for the third time.'

'Tell me, Mikhail,' Semyon asked, 'why did God punish you and what are those three truths, so that I too may know them?'

Mikhail replied, 'God punished me because I disobeyed Him. I was an angel of the Lord and I disobeyed Him. Yes, I was an angel in heaven and the Lord sent me down to earth to take a woman's soul. I flew down and saw the woman lying there. She was sick, all alone and had just given birth to twins, two little girls. There they were, crawling around their mother, but she was unable to put them to her breasts. When she saw me she understood that God had sent me to take her soul. She burst into tears and said, "Angel of the Lord! My husband has just been buried, killed by a falling tree. I have no sister, no aunt, no grandmother – no one to

bring up my little orphans. So please don't take my soul, let me suckle my babies, bring them up and set them on their feet. Children cannot live without father or mother!" And I did what she asked, pressed one little girl to her breast, put the other in her arms and ascended to heaven. I flew to God and told Him, "I could not bring myself to take the soul of a woman who had just borne twins. The father was killed by a falling tree and the mother had just given birth and begged me not to take her soul. 'Let me suckle my children, bring them up and set them on their feet. Children cannot live without a father or mother,' she pleaded. So I did not take that woman's soul." And then God said, "If you go down to earth and take that woman's soul you will discover three truths: you will learn *what dwells in man, what is not given to man* and *what men live by*. When you have learnt these truths you shall return to heaven." So I flew down to earth again and took the mother's soul. The babies dropped from her breasts and her body rolled over on to one of them, crushing its leg. Then I rose above the village, wishing to return her soul to God, but I was seized by a strong wind and my wings drooped and fell off. And so the soul alone returned to God and I fell to earth, by the roadside.'

11

And now Semyon and Matryona realized whom they had been clothing and feeding and had taken in to live with them. And they both wept for joy and fear. And the angel said, 'I was alone and naked in that field. Never before had

I known the needs of man, never had I known cold or hunger. But now I was an ordinary mortal, cold and hungry and not knowing what to do. And then I saw a chapel in the field, built for the glory of God. So I went to it to seek shelter. But it was locked and I could not enter. So I sat down behind it to shelter from the wind. Evening came and I was famished, freezing and in pain. Suddenly I heard a man coming down the road. He was carrying a pair of boots and talking to himself. For the first time since I became a man I saw the mortal face of man. It terrified me and I turned away. And I could hear this man wondering how to protect his body from the winter cold and feed his wife and children. And I thought, "I am perishing with cold and hunger, but here is someone whose only thought is how to find a warm coat for himself and his wife, and food for his family. I cannot expect any help from him." When the man saw me he frowned, looking even more terrifying, and he passed me by. I was desperate. But suddenly I heard him coming back. As I looked he no longer seemed the same man. Before, his face had borne the stamp of death, but now he had suddenly become alive again and in that face I could see God. He came up to me, clothed me and took me to his home. When we arrived a woman came out to meet us and she spoke. This woman was even more terrifying than the man. Her breath seemed to come from the grave and I was almost choked by that deathly stench. She wished to cast me out into the cold and I knew that if she did that she would die. Then suddenly her husband told her to think of God and at once she was transformed. When she had given us supper I returned the

look she gave me and saw that death no longer dwelt in her, but life. And in her too I could see God.

'And I recalled God's first lesson: *thou shalt learn what dwelleth in man*. And now I knew that it is Love that dwells in man. I was overjoyed that God had begun to reveal what He had promised to reveal, and I smiled for the first time. But I did not know the whole truth yet. I did not yet know what is not given to man and what men live by.

'And so I came to live with you and one year passed. One day a rich gentleman came to order a pair of boots that would last a year without splitting or losing their shape. When I looked at him I suddenly saw my comrade, the Angel of Death, standing behind him. No one but I could see that angel. And I knew that he would take the gentleman's soul before sunset. And I thought, "Here is a man who wants to provide for himself for a year from now but does not know that by evening he will be dead.' And so I remembered God's second lesson: *thou shalt learn what is* not *given to man*.

'What dwells in man I already knew. Now I knew that which is not given to man: it is not given to him to know his bodily needs. And I smiled for the second time. I rejoiced that I had seen my fellow angel and that God had revealed His second truth.

'But still I did not know everything. I did not understand what it is that men live by. And so I lived on, waiting for God to reveal this last truth to me. In my sixth year that woman came here with the two little girls. I recognized the girls and learnt how they had stayed alive. After this discovery I thought, "The mother pleaded with me for her children's sake

and I believed what she said, thinking that children cannot live without father or mother. But the other woman had nursed them and brought them up." And when I saw how much love this woman had for the children and how she wept over them I saw the living God in her and understood *what men live by*. And I realized that God had revealed His last lesson and had forgiven me. So I smiled for the third time.'

12

And the angel's body was bared and it was robed in light, so that the eye could not look upon it. And the angel's voice grew louder, as though it came not from him, but from heaven itself. And the angel said, 'I have learned that men live not by selfishness, but by love.

'It was not given to the mother to know what her children needed for their lives. Nor was it given to the rich man to know what his true needs were. Nor is it given to any man to know, before the sun has set, whether he will need boots for his living body or slippers for his corpse. When I became a mortal I survived not by thinking of myself, but through the love that dwelt in a passer-by and his wife, and the compassion and love they showed me. The two orphans' lives were preserved, not by what others may have intended for them, but by the love that dwelt in the heart of a woman, a complete stranger, and by the love and compassion she showed them. Indeed, all men live not by what they may intend for their own well-being, but by the love that dwells in others.

'Previously I had known that God gave life to men and desired that they should live. But then I came to know something else.

'I came to understand that God does not wish men to live apart and that is why He does not reveal to each man what he needs for himself *alone*. On the contrary, He wishes men to live in peace and harmony with each other and for this reason He has revealed to each and every one of them what *all* men need, as well as themselves.

'And I understood that men only think that they live by caring only about themselves: in reality they live by love alone. He who dwells in love dwells in God, and God in him, for God is love.'

And the angel sang the Lord's praises and the hut shook with the sound of his voice. And the roof parted and a pillar of fire rose from earth to heaven. Semyon and his wife and children prostrated themselves; the angel's wings unfurled and he soared into the sky.

When Semyon came to his senses the hut was just as it had always been and there was no one there but him and his family.

PENGUIN

LITTLE BLACK

CLASSICS

PENGUIN

LITTLE BLACK

CLASSICS

PENGUIN

LITTLE BLACK

CLASSICS

“‘已经跑了这么多，
现在停下来，
会被人家笑话的！’”

PENGUIN

LITTLE BLACK

CLASSICS

*此中文译本译自俄语原文

一个人需要许多土地吗？

How Much Land Does a Man Need?

［俄］列夫·托尔斯泰 著

草婴 译

中信出版集团 · 北京

图书在版编目（CIP）数据

企鹅经典·小黑书. 第一辑：英、汉 / (日) 吉田兼好等著；文东等译. -- 北京：中信出版社，2018.11（2022.7 重印）
书名原文：Penguin Little Black Classics
ISBN 978-7-5086-9400-9

Ⅰ. ①企… Ⅱ. ①吉… ②文… Ⅲ. ①世界文学—作品综合集—英、汉 Ⅳ. ①I11

中国版本图书馆 CIP 数据核字 (2018) 第 193780 号

How Much Land Does a Man Need
'How Much Land Does A Man Need?' and 'What Men Live By', published in their original Russian in 1836 and 1835 respectively. They are taken from How Much Land Does a Man Need? And Other Stories. This edition published in Penguin Classics 2015.

企鹅经典：小黑书　第一辑
一个人需要许多土地吗？

著　　者：[俄] 列夫·托尔斯泰
译　　者：草婴
出版发行：中信出版集团股份有限公司
　　　　　（北京市朝阳区惠新东街甲 4 号富盛大厦 2 座 邮编 100029）
承 印 者：河北鹏润印刷有限公司

开　　本：787mm×1092mm　1/32　　印　　张：41　　字　　数：300 千字
版　　次：2018 年 11 月第 1 版　　印　　次：2022 年 7 月第 13 次印刷
京权图字：01-2018-6477
书　　号：ISBN 978-7-5086-9400-9
定　　价：149.00 元（全 10 册）

服务热线：400-600-8099
投稿邮箱：author@citicpub.com

目录

一个人需要许多土地吗?

一

姐姐从城里来乡下看望妹妹。姐姐嫁了个城里商人，妹妹嫁了个乡下农民。姐妹俩喝着茶，谈着天。姐姐得意扬扬地吹嘘她在城里的生活：她的房子多么宽敞，衣服多么时髦，她的孩子打扮得多么漂亮，她吃得多么香，喝得多么美，她怎么乘马车兜风，上剧场看戏。

妹妹听了很生气，就竭力贬低商人的生活，美化农民的生活。

她说："我可不愿拿我的生活换你那种生活。尽管日子清苦，我们却无忧无虑。你们过得阔气，有时大发

其财，但有时亏个精光。常言道：赚钱、亏本是双胞胎。今天百万富翁，明天上街要饭。我们庄稼人要稳当得多。我们肚子里油水少，但是寿命长，我们发不了财，也饿不了肚子。”

姐姐说：“成天同猪牛打交道，肚子能吃得多饱？你们不懂得文明，不知道礼貌！不论你们当家的怎样累死累活，一辈子泡在猪粪牛尿里，永远没有出头的日子，你们的孩子也一样。”

妹妹说：“是的，我们干的就是这样的活儿，但日子过得踏实，我们不求人，也不怕谁。你们在城里到处受诱惑：今天太太平平，明天就会碰上魔鬼，引诱你们当家的去赌钱喝酒，嫖妓宿娼，到头来一场空。难道没有这样的事吗？”

当家的巴霍姆这时躺在炕上，听着她们闲聊。

“说得对，”他说道，“我们庄稼人从小种地，脑子从来不胡思乱想。只对一件事烦恼——地太少！要是有足够的土地，别说人，就是魔鬼也吓不倒我！”

姐妹俩喝完茶，又谈了一通衣着打扮，收拾好杯盘，躺下睡觉。

不料魔鬼坐在炕后面，这番话他听得一清二楚。魔

鬼感到高兴，因为农民老婆夸奖丈夫，说他要是有土地，就连魔鬼也不怕。

魔鬼想：“好吧，让我来跟你较量一下。我给你许多土地，就用土地来制服你。”

二

附近住着一个不大富裕的太太。她有一百二十俄亩[1]地。原来她跟农民相处得很好，她不欺负他们。后来她雇了一个退伍兵来当管家，他动不动就要罚农民款。尽管巴霍姆小心翼翼，还是常常出事，不是马冲进燕麦地，就是牛闯到花园里，再不就是牛犊践踏草地，他就只好被罚款。

巴霍姆付了罚款，就回家打骂老婆孩子。一个夏天，巴霍姆吃了这个管家许多苦。等到牲口圈起来过冬，他才放下心来，虽然得多费点儿饲料，但不用担惊受怕。

冬天，听说太太要出卖土地，大路上一家客店的老板想把它买下来。农民们听了都很恐慌。他们想：“要是客店老板买下这块地，他罚起款来一定比太太更厉害。

---

1. 一俄亩约合 1.09 公顷。（说明：书中脚注均为译者注。）

我们不能没有这块地，我们都靠它过活。”农民们就一起来到太太那里，要求她别把地卖给客店老板而卖给他们，他们愿意多出点儿钱。太太答应了。农民们商量由村社买下整块土地。他们商量了一次又一次，但始终没有谈成。原来是魔鬼在其中作怪，使他们的意见不能统一。最后农民们决定各人根据自己的力量各买各的，太太也答应了。巴霍姆听说邻居向太太买了二十俄亩地，太太答应先收一半钱，其余一半一年后再付。巴霍姆很羡慕，想：“地都被买光了，弄得我一无所有。”他就同妻子商量。

他说：“大家都在买地，我们也得买十来俄亩。要不管家动不动就罚款，我们没法儿过日子。”

他们考虑怎样设法买地。他们有一百卢布存款，卖掉一匹马驹和一半蜜蜂，把儿子抵押出去当雇工，再向连襟借点儿钱，这样就能凑满一半地价。

巴霍姆凑齐钱，看中一块地，有十五俄亩，带一片小树林，就去同太太谈。他们谈成了这笔买卖，拍了板，付了定金。他们又进城，把地契过了户，付了一半款子，其余一半两年内付清。

这样，巴霍姆就有了自己的土地。他借了种子，播

在他买来的土地上。庄稼长得很好。一年之内他就付清了太太的欠款，还了连襟的债。巴霍姆从此成了土地的主人：他耕种自己的地，在自己的地上割草，在自己的地上伐木，在自己的地上放牧牲口。不论翻耕自己的土地，还是观赏自己的作物或者草地，巴霍姆总是心花怒放。他总觉得他土地上的草长得特别茂盛，花开得格外美丽。以前他走过这片土地，觉得它同别的土地一样，但现在却觉得它完全与众不同。

三

巴霍姆这样过着日子，感到心满意足。只要邻居不来糟蹋他的庄稼和草地，就一切称心如意了。他恳求他们，但是没有用：一会儿牧人把牛放到他的草地上，一会儿夏天夜里放牧的马闯进他的庄稼地。巴霍姆总是把牲口赶走，原谅主人。他一直忍着不去告状，但后来实在受不了了，就告到乡里。他知道邻居这样做并不是有意的，而是因为土地太少，但又想："也不能听任不管，这样下去他们会把地糟蹋光的。得教训教训他们。"

他一次一次上法院告状，法院罚一两个农民赔偿。

邻居们对巴霍姆就怀恨在心，一再故意糟蹋他的地。有一天夜里他来到树林里，看见有十棵椴树被砍倒剥去树皮。巴霍姆来到树林里，看见有样东西白乎乎的。他骑马跑近一看，地上横着几棵椴树，旁边露出几个树桩。要是只砍去边上几棵倒也罢了，可是那坏蛋竟砍个精光。巴霍姆看了大为生气："哼，我要知道是谁干的，我就找他算账。"他想来想去，断定："不是别人，准是谢苗。"他走到谢苗家去找，什么也没有找到，两人只对骂了一通。他告到法院，谢苗被传去审问。法院一再审查，谢苗进行辩解，也没有找到罪证。巴霍姆越发生气，他跟乡长、法官都吵了嘴。

"你们包庇小偷。要是你们大公无私，就不会开脱小偷了。"

巴霍姆跟法官和左邻右舍都吵了嘴。有人威胁要烧他的房子。巴霍姆的地虽然多了，但他的日子却更加难过。

当时盛传有许多人迁移到新的地区去。巴霍姆想："我可不用离开我的土地，要是有人离开这儿，我们的地盘可以宽广些。我会把他们的地弄到手，把我的农庄扩大，这样日子就会更舒坦。要不总觉得土地太少。"

一天，巴霍姆坐在家里，来了一个过路的农民。巴

霍姆留他在家里过夜，给他饭吃，同他谈天，问他从什么地方来。农民说，他从伏尔加河下游来，他在那里当雇工。谈着谈着，农民说，有许多人迁移到那里，他们就在那里定居，加入村社，每人分到十俄亩地。

他说："那边的地很肥，种下黑麦，麦秆长得比马背还高，可茂盛了，五把就可以扎一大捆。有个农民很穷，去的时候只有一双手，如今已有六匹马、两头牛了。"

巴霍姆心动了。他想："既然有好日子可过，何必在这里受穷？我把这里的地和房子都卖掉，到那边另起炉灶，大干一番。挤在这小地方真是活受罪。不过我得亲自去了解了解。"

他在初夏动身，乘轮船沿伏尔加河到萨马拉，然后步行四百俄里[1]到达目的地。情况果然如此。农民的地很多，每人分到十俄亩，他们高高兴兴加入村社。谁要是有钱，除了份地外还可以买地，最好的地每俄亩只要三卢布，要多少可以买多少！

巴霍姆把情况了解清楚后，秋天回家把东西变卖一空。他带点儿赚头卖掉土地，又卖掉房子和牲口，退出村社。开春就全家搬到了新地方去。

1. 一俄里约合 1.0668 公里。

四

巴霍姆带着一家人来到新地方，参加了一个大村的村社。他招待村社长辈喝酒，弄到了各种证件。村社接受巴霍姆入社，分给他五十俄亩份地，分在几个地方，牧场是公用的。巴霍姆盖了房子，养了牲口。单是从村社分到的地就比原来的多两倍，而且都是种庄稼的沃土。日子过得比原来好十倍。饲料也很充裕，牲口要养多少就可以养多少。

巴霍姆在这里安顿下来，感到称心如意，但定居后，又觉得土地不够。第一年，巴霍姆在份地上种小麦，收成很好。他种小麦来了劲，但觉得地不够。刚种过的地不宜立刻再种。当地人在熟荒地和休闲地上种小麦，种了一两年就让土地休闲，长野草。这种地要的人很多，不够分配，为此常常发生争吵。有钱的自己种，穷人则把地租给商人，租金用来缴税。巴霍姆想多种些，第二年就去向商人租来一块地，一年为期。他种得更多，收成更好，但那块地离家太远，赶车得走十五俄里。他看到有些农民兼做买卖，自己有农庄，日子过得很阔气。

巴霍姆想：“我要是也买点儿私地，办个农庄，就更称心如意了。”巴霍姆开始考虑怎样买私地。

巴霍姆这样过了三年。他租地种小麦，年年风调雨顺，小麦喜获丰收，钱越存越多。这样的日子本可以一直过下去，但他感到麻烦，因为年年得为租地奔走忙碌，什么地方有好地，农民就涌到那里，把地一抢而光。你去晚了，就没有地种。第三年，他同一个商人向农民合买一片牧场，农民已耕了地，可是有纠纷，农民们告到官府，地也就白耕了。他想：“如果那地是自己的，就不用向人打躬作揖，也不会有麻烦了。”

巴霍姆到处打听哪里可以买到私地。他遇到一个农民，向他买了五百俄亩地，那人破产了，所以卖得很便宜。巴霍姆同他讨价还价，谈了半天，最后以一千五百卢布成交，一半付现金。这事差不多已办成，不想有个商人路过他那里喂马。巴霍姆同他一起喝茶，谈天。商人讲到他从遥远的巴什基尔来。他说，他向巴什基尔人买了五千俄亩地，总共才花了一千卢布。巴霍姆就向他详细打听这事。商人说：“不过先得去巴结老人。我花一百卢布买了绸袍、地毯送给他们，再加一箱茶叶，把能喝酒的都请来喝酒。结果我就以每俄亩二十戈比的价钱成

交了。”他出示地契说，“地都在河边，上面长满茅草。”

巴霍姆又详细打听了一番。

商人说：“那边的土地一年也走不到头，全是巴什基尔人的。巴什基尔人像羊一样没有脑子，那里的地几乎可以白拿。”

巴霍姆想：“既然如此，我何必花一千五百卢布去买五百俄亩地，还要欠债！我拿一千卢布到那边可以买到多少地啊！”

五

巴霍姆问清了到那地方的路径。他送走商人就准备动身。他抛下家给妻子照管，自己带了一名雇工出发。他们来到城里，照商人的话买了一箱茶叶、礼品和酒。他们走啊走啊，一连走了大约五百俄里，第七天来到巴什基尔人的游牧地。一切就像商人所说的那样，巴什基尔人临河搭了毡帐篷，住在草原上。他们不种地，也不吃粮。草原上放着成群的牛马。马驹拴在帐篷后面，母马一天两次被牵来喂奶。他们挤马奶，做马奶酒。巴什基尔女人搅马奶酒，做干酪，男人只知道喝马奶酒，饮

茶，吃羊肉，吹笛子。他们个个肥肥胖胖，快快活活，整个夏天就像过节一样不干活儿。他们愚昧无知，不懂俄语，但是和蔼可亲。

巴什基尔人一看见巴霍姆从帐篷里出来，就把他团团围住。他们找来一名翻译。巴霍姆对他们说，他是来看地的。巴什基尔人听了很高兴，把巴霍姆领到一个最好的帐篷里，让他坐在地毯上，又给了他羽绒靠枕。他们围坐在四周，请他饮茶，喝马奶酒。巴什基尔人还宰了一头羊，请他吃羊肉。巴霍姆从马车里取出礼品，分送给他们。巴霍姆送了巴什基尔人礼品，又把茶叶分给他们。巴什基尔人很高兴，彼此叽里咕噜地说了一通，然后叫翻译告诉巴霍姆。

翻译说："他们说，他们喜欢你，我们这里的风俗是尽量让客人高兴，还要回赠礼品。你送了我们礼品，现在你说说，你喜欢我们这里什么东西，我们好给你还礼。"

"我最喜欢你们这里的土地，"巴霍姆说，"我们那里地少，而且种薄了，你们这里地多，而且很肥。这样好的地我还从没见过呢。"

翻译翻译了他的话。巴什基尔人又交谈了好一阵。巴霍姆不明白他们在说些什么，但看出他们很高兴，又

是叫，又是笑。随后他们安静下来，望着巴霍姆，翻译就说：“他们要我对你说，他们愿意给你土地来回报你的好意，你要多少给你多少。你只要用手点一点，那地就是你的了。”

他们又谈了一会儿，像是在争论什么问题。巴霍姆问他们在争论什么，翻译说：“有人说，土地的事得问问头人，没得到他的许可不行。也有人说，没得到他的许可也可以。”

六

巴什基尔人争论着，突然来了个戴狐皮帽的人。大家都不说话，站起来。翻译说：“这位就是头人。”

巴霍姆立刻拿出一件最好的绸袍送给头人，还给了他五磅茶叶。头人接受了礼物，在首席坐下。巴什基尔人立刻对头人说着什么。头人听着听着，点了点头，告诉他们不用再说下去。然后他用俄语对巴霍姆说话。

“好吧，”他说，“你喜欢什么地方，就拿什么地方。地多的是。”

“我怎么才能把要的地都拿到手呢？”巴霍姆想，

“总得有个保证啊。要不现在说是我的，以后又把地收回去。”

“谢谢你们的美意，”巴霍姆说，“你们的地很多，我要的不多。不过我要知道给我的地是哪一块。总得量一下，给我定下来。要不死生由命，现在你们这些好人给了我土地，但难保将来你们的子孙不收回去。”

“你说的有理，”头人说，“可以定下来。”

巴霍姆说：“我听说有个商人来过你们这儿，你们也给了他地，还写了契约，我也希望这样做。”

头人懂得他的意思。

“这都不成问题，”他说，“我们这儿有文书。我们到城里去一次，正式订个契约。”

“那么价钱怎么算？”巴霍姆问。

“我们这儿只有一个价：一千卢布一天。”

巴霍姆不懂他的意思。

“一天是多少啊？一天等于几俄亩？”

“我们不会算，”他说，“我们出卖土地用天计算；你一天能绕多少地，这些地就归你，价钱是一千卢布一天。”

巴霍姆感到惊讶，他说：“一天走下来，那地可多啦！”

头人笑起来。

“全部归你！”头人说，“但有一个条件：你要是当天不能回到出发的地方，你的钱就白花了。”

“那我怎么在走过的地方做记号？”巴霍姆问。

“我们将站在你看中的地方，你去绕一圈，随身带一把铲子，你要什么地方，就挖个坑盖上草做记号，我们再从一个坑到另一个坑犁出一条沟。你要绕多大的圈子，就绕多大的圈子，但日落之前一定要回到出发的地方。你一圈绕下来的地方都归你所有。”

巴霍姆高兴极了。他们决定第二天一早出发。接着大家又谈天，又喝马奶酒，又吃羊肉，又饮茶，直到天黑。他们安排巴霍姆睡羽绒褥子，讲定天一亮就集合，日出前出发，这才各自回家。

七

巴霍姆躺在羽绒褥子上睡不着，心里一直在想：“我要弄到一大块地。我一天可以走五十俄里路。现在日长，五十俄里绕一圈地可多啦。以后我把坏地卖掉，或者让给农民，挑最好的地自己种。我要买两头公牛，雇两名工人。我要种五十俄亩地，其余的养草放牲口。”

巴霍姆通宵没有合眼，直到天快亮才迷迷糊糊地睡着。他做了个梦，梦见他就躺在这个帐篷里，听见外面有人在哈哈大笑。他想看看谁在笑，就起身走出帐篷，看见巴什基尔头人坐在帐篷前捧腹大笑。他走过去问道：“你在笑什么呀？”他发现这人不是巴什基尔头人，而是几天前路过他家告诉他买地的商人。他刚问商人：“你来这儿好久了？”立刻又发现他不是商人，而是那个好久前从伏尔加河下游来的农民。接着巴霍姆又看见那不是农民，而是一个长着犄角和蹄子的魔鬼。魔鬼坐在那里哈哈大笑，前面躺着个只穿短衫裤的赤脚农民。巴霍姆仔细瞧瞧，才发现这是个死人，而且就是他自己。巴霍姆吓醒了，想：“真是什么梦都会做啊！”他回头一看，看见门外天色已经发白。他想：“得叫醒人，是时候了。”巴霍姆起身，叫醒车上的雇工，吩咐他套车，自己则去唤醒巴什基尔人。

“起来吧，到草原上去量地。”他说。

巴什基尔人纷纷起来，聚集在一起，头人也来了。巴什基尔人又喝马奶酒，还要请巴霍姆饮茶，但巴霍姆等不及了。

“要走就走吧，是时候了。”他说。

八

巴什基尔人集合起来，有的骑马，有的坐车，大家出发。巴霍姆跟他的雇工带了铲子，坐上自己的马车上路。他们来到草原上，朝霞刚刚出现。他们爬上一座小丘。大家下了车，下了马，聚在一起。头人走到巴霍姆跟前，用手指着说："瞧，这片土地都是我们的，一眼望不到边。你随便挑吧。"

巴霍姆眼睛红了：这是一片熟荒地，平得像手掌，黑得像鸦片，洼地上野草丛生，长得齐胸高。

头人摘下狐皮帽放在地上，说："瞧，这就是记号。你从这儿出发，再回到这儿。凡是你绕一圈走下来的地都归你。"

巴霍姆摸出钱放在帽子上，脱下长袍，只穿一件短袄，收紧宽腰带，把一袋面包揣在怀里，又把水壶挂在腰带上，拉拉靴筒，向雇工要了铲子，准备上路。他反复考虑走哪个方向，觉得到处都是好地。他想："反正都一样，我朝太阳升起的地方走就是了。"他面对太阳站着，活动活动身子，等太阳从天边出来。他想："不能浪

费时间，要趁凉快赶路。”等太阳从地平线一出来，巴霍姆就背起铲子向草原走去。

巴霍姆走得不快不慢。他走了一俄里光景停下来站住，挖了一个坑，盖上草皮，这样醒目些。接着又向前走。他活动活动身子，加快脚步。他走了一段路，又挖了一个坑。

巴霍姆回头望了望。小丘在阳光下看得清清楚楚，人们站在那里，马车的轮子闪闪发亮。巴霍姆估计他已走了五俄里。他感到热，脱下短袄搭在肩上，继续往前走。又走了五俄里的样子。天气更热了。他望望太阳，已是吃早饭的时候。

“已经走了一程[1]，”巴霍姆想，“不过一天能走四程路，回去还早。让我把靴子脱掉。”他坐下来脱下靴子挂在腰带上，继续走路。现在比较轻松了。他想：“让我再走五俄里，然后往左拐。这地方太好了，放弃可惜。越往前，地越好。”他又一直走过去。他回头一看，小丘隐约可见，小丘上的人像黑蚂蚁，还有一样东西在发亮。

巴霍姆想：“是啊，这个方向已走了不少路，得拐弯了。可把我渴死了，真想喝点儿水。”他停下来，挖了个

1. 一程指马一口气能走的路。

更大的坑，盖上草皮，解下水壶，喝了个够，就陡然向左拐弯。他走啊走，草长得更高，天更热了。

巴霍姆走累了。他望望太阳，已是吃午饭的时候。他想:“好吧，让我歇会儿。”巴霍姆收住脚步，蹲下来。他吃了点儿面包，又喝了点儿水，但没有躺下。他想:“我一躺下就会睡着的。”他坐了一会儿，继续往前走。起初走得还轻松，因为吃了点儿东西，添了力气。天气越来越热，他直想打瞌睡，但他没有停下来，心里想，忍耐一时，享福一世。

他朝这个方向又走了许多路，正想向左拐，忽然看见一片水洼地，觉得放弃可惜。他想:“这里种亚麻很好。”他又一直向前走去。他走过水洼地，在那边挖了一个坑，拐了弯。巴霍姆回头望望小丘，那边热得雾气弥漫，仿佛空气也在颤动，隐约看得见小丘上的人，离他大约有十五俄里。巴霍姆想:“哦，那两边走得够多了，这边得少走些。”他加快脚步朝第三个方向走去。他望望太阳，太阳已到中天，可第三个方向还只走了两俄里。距离出发的地方仍有十五俄里。他想:“不行，虽然这样我会弄到一块斜形地，但是必须笔直赶回去。我不要更多的地，现在已经很多了。”巴霍姆急忙挖了一个坑，拐

弯笔直向小丘走去。

九

巴霍姆一直向小丘走去。他汗流浃背，两脚划破，浑身瘫软。他想歇一会儿，但是不能，日落之前要赶不回去的。太阳不等人，越来越往下沉，往下沉。他想：“哦，我是不是要的太多了？会不会来不及？”他往前望望小丘，望望太阳：离出发点很远，而太阳离地平线却不远了。

巴霍姆一直走着，越来越吃力，但仍不断加快脚步。他走啊走啊，离终点还是很远。他小跑起来。他抛下短袄、靴子、水壶和帽子，只拿着铲子当拐杖。他想：“唉，我太贪心，这下子全完了。日落以前我跑不到了。”他心里发慌，更加上气不接下气。巴霍姆跑得浑身大汗，衬衫衬裤都贴在身上，嘴巴发干。他的胸膛好像铁匠铺里的风箱一样拼命喘气，心上好像有一把铁锤在敲打，两腿失去知觉，好像散了架。巴霍姆感到害怕，心里想：“可别累死啊。”

他怕死，但又不愿停下来。他想：“已经跑了这么多，

现在停下来，会被人家笑话的。”他跑啊跑啊，越来越接近终点，他听见巴什基尔人在向他大声叫喊，心里更加发慌。他拼出最后的力气向前跑去，太阳已接近地平线，落到迷雾中，它又大又红，像血染了一样，眼看就要落下去了。太阳离地平线很近，他到达出发点也不远了。巴霍姆已看见小丘上人们在向他招手，要他加油。他看见地上的狐皮帽，看见帽子上的钱；他看见头人坐在地上，双手按住肚子。巴霍姆想起了他的梦，同时想：“土地很多，但上帝是不是让我在上面过？唉，我把自己给毁了，我跑不到了。”

巴霍姆望望太阳，太阳已触到地平线，一半已隐没不见，只剩下一半。巴霍姆竭尽全力冲去，两只脚勉强跟上，使自己不致倒下。巴霍姆跑近小丘，天色突然黑下来。他回头一看，太阳已经落山了。巴霍姆大叫一声，想：“我白费力气了。”他想停下来，但听见巴什基尔人还在叫喊。他突然想到，他从低处看太阳已经落下，但从小丘上看太阳一定还没有落下。他拼着最后一口气跑上小丘。小丘上还很亮。巴霍姆跑上去，看见了帽子。帽子前面坐着头人，双手捧腹哈哈笑着。巴霍姆想起了那个梦，他惊叫一声，两腿一软扑倒在地，他的手伸出

去够着了帽子。

“啊，真是条好汉！”头人叫道，“你得到了许多土地！”

巴霍姆的雇工跑过来，想把他扶起，但他口吐鲜血，躺在地上死了。

巴什基尔人叹息不已。

雇工拿起铲子给巴霍姆挖了一个坑，从头到脚有三俄尺[1]长，就把他埋了。

---

1. 一俄尺合 0.71 米。

人靠什么生活

我们因为爱弟兄，就晓得是已经出生入死了。没有爱心的，仍住在死中。(《新约·约翰一书》，第三章，第十四节)

凡有世上财物的，看见弟兄穷乏，却塞住怜恤的心，爱上帝的心怎能存在他里面呢？（同上，第三章，第十七节）

小子们哪，我们相爱，不要只在言语和舌头上，总要在行为和诚实上。(同上，第三章，第十八节)

爱是从上帝来的，凡有爱心的，都是由上帝而生，并且认识上帝。（同上，第四章，第七节）

没有爱心的，就不认识上帝，因为上帝就是爱。（同上，第四章，第八节）

从来没有人见过上帝。我们若彼此相爱，上帝就住在我们里面。（同上，第四章，第十二节）

上帝就是爱。住在爱里面的，就是住在上帝里面，上帝也住在他里面。（同上，第四章，第十六节）

人若说，我爱上帝却恨他的弟兄，就是说谎话的。不爱他所看见的弟兄，就不能爱没有看见的上帝。（同上，第四章，第二十节）

一

从前有个鞋匠，他带着老婆、孩子租了农民的一所小房子，住在那里。他没有自己的房子，没有土地，靠

做鞋养家糊口。粮食贵，工钱贱，挣得的钱全部吃光。夫妻俩只有一件皮袄，而且这件皮袄也已穿得破破烂烂。鞋匠想买一块羊皮做件新皮袄，为此他已攒了一年多的钱。

到今年秋天，鞋匠已攒了一些钱；老婆箱子里藏着一张三卢布钞票，还有五卢布二十戈比是村里农民欠他的债。

一天早晨，鞋匠打算去村里买羊皮。他在衬衫外面穿上老婆的布棉袄，外面再套一件布长袍，口袋里放着那张三卢布钞票。他折了一根棍子，吃过早饭就动身。他想："我从农民那里收来五卢布，再加上自己的三卢布，就可以买一块羊皮做新皮袄了。"

鞋匠来到村里，走进一个农民家，农民出去了，他老婆没钱，但答应一星期内叫丈夫送去。他去找另一个农民，那农民指天发誓说他没有钱，只付了二十戈比修鞋费。鞋匠想赊一块羊皮，可是卖皮货的信不过他。

"拿钱来，"他说，"皮子随你挑，我可尝过讨债的滋味。"

结果鞋匠一事无成，只收到二十戈比修鞋钱，还有一双旧毡靴，那是一个农民要他拿回去用皮子码边的。

鞋匠垂头丧气，拿二十戈比全喝了伏特加，空着一双手回家。早晨，鞋匠感到寒冷彻骨，但喝了点儿酒，不穿皮袄也还暖和。鞋匠走大路回家，一手拿棍子敲着冰冻的地面，一手摇摇晃晃提着毡靴，嘴里自言自语：“我不穿皮袄也挺暖和。一杯酒下肚，浑身发热，皮袄都用不着了。我现在高高兴兴回家去。嗨，我就是这样一个人！有什么可烦恼的？没有皮袄照样活下去。我一辈子也用不着皮袄，可是老太婆会不高兴的。再说，你整天给人干活儿，却一个钱也拿不到，总叫人生气。哼，你要是不拿钱来，我就摘你帽子，真的，摘你帽子。要不这像什么话？一次只给你二十戈比！哼，二十戈比能干什么？只能喝一盅。他说他手头紧。你手头紧，我就不紧？你有房子，有牲口，什么都有。你有自己种的粮，可我得花钱买粮吃。不论怎么说，我光买面包每星期就得三卢布。我回去，家里没有面包，又得掏出一个半卢布去买。所以你得把欠的钱还我。”

这时鞋匠来到大路转角处的一座小教堂旁。他看见教堂那边有个白乎乎的东西。天已黑下来，鞋匠仔细看了半天，也看不清究竟是什么。他想：“石头吗？这里没有这样的石头。牲口吗？又不像牲口。脑袋有点儿像人，

但怎么会是白乎乎的？再说，人怎么会待在那里？”

他走近些，看清楚了。真稀奇，的确是一个人，但不知是死是活，光着身子坐在那里，身子靠在教堂墙上，一动不动。鞋匠很害怕，心里想：“准是谁杀了他，剥去衣服，把他扔在这里。我要是再走近点儿，就脱不了干系啦。”

鞋匠从旁边绕过去，走到教堂后面就看不见那个人了。他走过教堂，回头一看，那人已不再靠着墙壁，身子在动，仿佛也瞧着他。鞋匠越发害怕，心里想：“走过去，还是绕开？走过去，难保不出事，谁知道他是什么人？他落到这里准不是什么好事。要是走过去，他跳起来掐我的脖子，我就别想脱身了。即使他不掐脖子，你能拿一个光身子的人怎么办？总不能把自己身上最后一件衣服脱给他吧。上帝保佑！”

鞋匠加快脚步，眼看就要绕过教堂，但他的良心不答应。

鞋匠在路上站住。

“谢苗，你这算什么呀？”他自己对自己说，“人家遭难都快死了，你却害怕，想绕过去。难道你发了大财，怕人家抢你的钱吗？唉，谢苗，这样可不好！”

谢苗转身向那人走去。

二

谢苗走到那人身边，仔细一看，发现他年轻力壮，身上没有伤痕，但是几乎冻僵了。这可把他吓坏了。那人斜靠在墙上，眼睛不看谢苗，样子非常虚弱，连眼皮也抬不起来。谢苗走到他跟前，那人仿佛突然清醒过来，转过头，睁开眼睛，瞧了瞧谢苗。他的目光引起谢苗的爱怜。谢苗把毡靴往地上一扔，解下腰带放在毡靴上，然后脱下长袍。

“你不用说什么！”谢苗说，“快穿上！来！”

谢苗抓住那人的手肘，扶他站起来。那人站了起来。谢苗看到他身体细长、干净，手脚完整，相貌和蔼可亲。谢苗把长袍披在他肩上，可是他的手臂伸不进衣袖。谢苗把他的手塞进衣袖里，给他掩上前襟，束好腰带。

谢苗摘下破便帽，想给那人戴上，但自己头上感到冷。他想：“我的头全秃了，他却有一头长长的鬈发。”于是他又戴上帽子，“还是给他穿上靴子吧。”

谢苗让他坐下，给他穿上毡靴。

谢苗给他穿好衣服说:“好了，兄弟。你活动活动身子，暖和暖和。别的我就不管了。你能走吗？”

那人站在那里，温柔地瞧着谢苗，但说不出话来。

“你怎么不说话？总不能在这里过冬啊。得到有人家的地方去。喏，把我的棍子拿去，你身子虚，就拄着棍子走。打起精神来！”

那人就迈开步子。他走得挺轻松，没有落后。

他们在大路上走着，谢苗问:“你是哪里人？”

“我不是本地人。”

“本地人我都认识。你怎么会到教堂这儿来的？”

“我不能告诉你。”

“是不是有人欺负你了？”

“谁也没有欺负我。是上帝惩罚我。”

“当然，一切都是上帝的旨意，但你总得找个地方安顿啊。你要上哪儿去？”

“我都无所谓。”

谢苗听了觉得奇怪。那人不像个泼皮，说话也挺温和，可自己的事却绝口不谈。谢苗想:“天下什么怪事没有啊。”接着就对他说:“好吧，你就到我家去吧，哪怕去暖和暖和身子也好。”

谢苗向家里走去，陌生人跟在他旁边。起风了，谢苗穿着衬衫感到冷，他已酒意全消，身体都快冻僵了。他走着，吸着鼻子，掩紧身上的女短袄，想：“哼，买皮袄，买皮袄，回来连长袍都没有了，还带回一个光身男子。玛特廖娜准会不高兴的！”一想到玛特廖娜，谢苗就很担忧。他望望陌生人，记起那人在教堂旁的目光，心里感到一阵温暖。

三

谢苗的妻子一早就料理好家务。她劈了柴，打了水，让孩子们吃饱，自己也吃了点儿东西，坐着想心事。她在考虑，面包今天做还是明天做？家里还剩有一大块面包。

她想：“谢苗要是在那里吃了中饭，晚饭就吃不了多少，面包就够明天吃了。”

玛特廖娜反复掂着那块面包的重量，想：“今天不做面包吧。面粉只够烤一炉面包了，我们得熬到星期五。”

玛特廖娜收拾好面包，坐到桌子旁给丈夫补衬衫。她一面补，一边想着丈夫，不知他会买一块怎样的羊皮

回来。

“他可别被卖皮的骗了。我男人实在是个老实人。他从来不骗人，可是连小孩子都会让他上当。八卢布不是个小数目，可以做一件好皮袄。就算不是熟皮，也总是一件皮袄。去年冬天没有皮袄可难过啦！去河边不行，去哪儿都不行。他出门把衣服都穿走，我就没有衣服穿了。他今天出门不算早，但也该回来了。我这个老头子总不会去喝酒吧？”

玛特廖娜刚想到这里，台阶上就响起吱吱嘎嘎的声音，有人走进来。她把针插好，看见进来的有两个人：谢苗和一个汉子，那汉子光着头，脚上却穿着毡靴。

玛特廖娜立刻闻到丈夫身上酒气熏天。她想：“哼，真的喝过酒了。”她看见他身上没有穿长袍，只有一件女短袄，空着一双手，一声不吭，显出一副畏畏缩缩的样子，她的心都凉了。她想：“他准是把钱都喝光了，同这种浪荡汉鬼混，还把他带回家来。”

玛特廖娜让他们走进屋，自己也跟着进去。她发现这个陌生人年纪很轻，瘦瘦的，身上穿着他们家的长袍。长袍里没有衬衫，头上没戴帽子。他一进来，就垂下眼睛，一动不动地站着。玛特廖娜想，看来不是个正经人，

这么鬼鬼祟祟的。

玛特廖娜皱起眉头，走到灶边，冷眼看他们怎么样。

谢苗摘下帽子，规规矩矩地坐到长凳上。

“哎，玛特廖娜，”谢苗说，“给我们吃晚饭吧！”

玛特廖娜低声嘀咕着。她一动不动地站在灶旁，一会儿看看这个，一会儿望望那个，不住地摇头。谢苗看到老婆不高兴，但他无可奈何。他装作没注意，拉起陌生人的手说：“坐吧，兄弟，我们吃饭吧。”

陌生人在长凳上坐下。

“怎么，饭还没做吗？”

玛特廖娜火冒三丈。

“做了，可不是为你做的。我看你是喝糊涂了。你出去买皮袄，可回来连长袍也没有了，还带来一个光身子的无赖。我这儿没有你们酒鬼吃的饭！”

“够了，玛特廖娜，别胡说八道！你得先问问他是个什么人……”

“你说说，钱到哪儿去了？”

谢苗伸手到长袍口袋里，掏出钞票，把它们摊开来。

“钱在这里，特里丰诺夫没给钱，他答应明天给。”

玛特廖娜特别生气的是，他没有买皮袄，把最后一

件长袍给了一个光身子的人，还把他领回家来。

她一把抓住桌上的钞票，把它们藏好，说：“我没有晚饭。光身子的酒鬼太多了，喂不过来。”

“喂，玛特廖娜，别乱说。先听听人家……”

“酒鬼的傻话我可听够了。是的，我当初就不肯嫁给你这个酒鬼。妈妈给我的麻布被你喝掉了，这回买皮袄的钱又被你喝掉了。”

谢苗要向妻子解释他只喝掉二十戈比，他要说明他在哪儿找到这个人，但玛特廖娜不让他插嘴。她喋喋不休地说个没完，连十年前的旧账都翻了出来。

玛特廖娜说着说着，突然冲到谢苗跟前，抓住他的衣袖。

“还我的短袄。我只剩下这么一件衣服，你还要从我身上剥去，穿到自己身上。拿来，癞皮狗，叫你不得好死！”

谢苗从身上脱下短袄，把一个衣袖翻了过来，玛特廖娜一扯，把线脚都扯开了。玛特廖娜抓住短袄套到头上，走到门口。她想出去，但又站住。她怒气冲天，很想发作，但又想知道来的是个什么人。

四

玛特廖娜在门口站住说:“他要是个好人，也不会光着身子，可他连衬衫都不穿一件。他要是干的正经事，你也得说说从哪儿弄来这样一个花花公子。”

“对，我正要告诉你。我在路上看见这个人光着身子坐在教堂旁，完全冻僵了。又不是夏天，怎么能光着身子？上帝让我碰上他，要不他会冻死的。咳，叫我怎么办？天知道他会怎么样！我就把他拉起来，给他穿上衣服，带回家来。你别这样发火，玛特廖娜，罪过啊！我们都是凡人，有一天都要死的。”

玛特廖娜正要破口大骂，但看了陌生人一眼，就不作声了。陌生人坐在凳子边上，一动不动。他的双手放在膝盖上，头垂在胸前，眼睛闭着，眉头皱紧，仿佛喘不过气来。玛特廖娜没作声。谢苗说:“玛特廖娜，难道你心里没有上帝吗?！”

玛特廖娜听见这话，又瞧了陌生人一眼，她的心肠顿时软了下来。她从门边走到灶旁，端出晚饭。她把碗放在桌上，倒了一碗格瓦斯，拿出最后一块面包，又给了陌生人刀和匙子。

“您吃吧！”她说。

谢苗推了推陌生人说：“坐吧，年轻人！”

谢苗切了面包，把它撕碎，吃起来。玛特廖娜坐在桌子角上，一只手托着脑袋，望着陌生人。

玛特廖娜可怜陌生人，对他产生了好感。陌生人也突然高兴起来，不再皱眉头，抬眼望望玛特廖娜，微微一笑。

他们吃完晚饭，女主人收拾好餐桌，问陌生人：“你是哪里人？”

“我不是本地人。”

“你是怎么流落街头的？”

“我不能说。”

“是不是有谁抢劫了你？”

“是上帝惩罚我。”

“你就这样光着身子躺在那儿吗？”

“就这样光着身子躺在那儿，我冻坏了。谢苗看见我，可怜我，把身上的长袍脱下来给我穿上，叫我到这儿来。到了这儿，你也可怜我，给我吃，给我喝。上帝保佑你们！”

玛特廖娜站起来，从窗上取下她刚补好的谢苗的旧

衬衫递给陌生人，还找出一条裤子给他穿。

“拿去吧，我看你身上没有衬衣。你穿上，爱睡哪儿就睡哪儿，睡阁楼也行，睡炕也行。”

陌生人脱下长袍，穿上衬衫和裤子，躺到阁楼上。玛特廖娜熄了灯，拿起长袍，爬到丈夫身边。

玛特廖娜拿长袍一角盖在身上躺下来，但是睡不着，脑子里一直想着陌生人。

她想到，最后一块面包让他吃掉，他们明天就没有面包了。她想到，她给了他衬衫和裤子，心里闷闷不乐。可她想到他的微笑，心里便高兴了。

玛特廖娜好久都没有睡着，她听见谢苗也没有睡着，把长袍往他那边拉。

“谢苗！”

“嗯！”

“面包都吃光了，可我没发面。我不知道明天怎么过。是不是去向邻居玛拉尼雅借一点儿？”

“活一天是一天，不会挨饿的。”

老婆又躺了一会儿，不再作声。

“看样子他是个好人，只是干吗不肯讲他的来历？”

“大概不便说吧。”

“谢苗！”

“嗯！”

“我们给人家东西，可是怎么没有人给我们东西啊？”

谢苗不知道怎么回答，他只说：“别啰唆了！”他转了个身，睡着了。

五

第二天早晨谢苗醒来，孩子们还睡着，妻子向邻居借面包去了。那个陌生人穿着旧裤旧衬衫独自坐在长凳上，眼睛向上望。他的气色比昨天好。

谢苗说：“朋友，肚子饿了要吃面包，身子光着要穿衣服。人得养活自己。你会干什么活儿？”

“我什么也不会。”

谢苗感到奇怪，就说：“只要肯学，什么都学得会的。”

“人家都在干活儿，我也要干。”

“你叫什么名字？”

“米哈伊尔。”

“那么，米哈伊尔，你不愿谈自己，这随你的便，但你得养活自己。你要是能照我的话做，我就养你。”

“上帝保佑你，我愿意学。你教我怎么干就行。”

谢苗拿起纱，把它绕在手指上捻。

“你瞧，这事并不难……”

米哈伊尔瞧了一会儿，也把纱绕在手指上捻了起来。

谢苗教他给纱线上蜡。米哈伊尔立刻懂了。谢苗又教他把鬃毛捻到纱线上，怎样上靴子。米哈伊尔也立刻学会了。

不论谢苗教他做什么，他都一学就会。第三天他开始独自干活儿，仿佛做了一辈子的鞋。他干活儿不休息，吃得又少。工作间歇，他不说话，眼睛望着天空。他不上街，不闲聊，也不开玩笑。

只有第一天晚上，玛特廖娜给他吃晚饭，他才微微笑了笑。

六

日子过了一天又一天，过了一周又一周，不觉已过了一年。米哈伊尔仍在谢苗家干活儿。他的名声传开了：他做的靴子又挺括又结实，谁也比不上。附近一带的人都来找谢苗定做靴子，他的日子越过越富裕。

冬季的一天，谢苗和米哈伊尔正在干活儿，有一辆带铃铛的三驾雪橇向他家驶来。他们向窗外一望，看见雪橇在门口停下，一个汉子从驭座上下来，打开雪橇门。一位老爷身穿皮大衣，走下雪橇。他下了雪橇，走到谢苗家门口。玛特廖娜连忙起来打开门。老爷低下头走进小屋，又挺直身子，脑袋差点儿碰到天花板。他高大的身子把屋角都塞满了。

谢苗站起来鞠了一躬，看到老爷觉得很奇怪。他从没见过这样的人。谢苗自己筋脉毕露，米哈伊尔皮包骨头，玛特廖娜像一片木板，而这位老爷却像来自另一个世界：面色红润，体格魁梧，脖子粗得像公牛。他的整个身体就像用生铁铸成的。

老爷气喘吁吁，脱下皮大衣，坐在凳子上说："谁是鞋匠老板？"

谢苗走过去说："是我，老爷。"

老爷对他的跟班吆喝道："喂，费杰卡，拿皮子来。"

跟班跑进来，拿来一个包裹。老爷接过包裹，把它放在桌上。"解开来。"他说。跟班解开包裹。

老爷用一根手指戳戳皮子，对谢苗说："喂，听我说，鞋匠，你看见皮子了吗？"

“看见了，”谢苗说，“老爷。”

“那你知道这是什么皮子吗？”

谢苗摸摸皮子，说：“皮子挺好。”

“对，挺好！你这傻瓜还没见过这样的皮子吧。这是德国货，我花二十卢布买来的。”

谢苗吓了一跳，说：“我们哪里见过。”

“对了，一点儿不错。你能用这块皮子给我做一双靴子吗？”

“能，老爷。”

“这就对了。你要明白，你这是给谁做靴子，用的是什么皮子。我要你替我做一双靴子，穿上一年不走样、不开线。你能，就拿去裁；你不能，就别动。我把丑话说在前头：要是不到一年靴子开线、走样，我叫你坐班房；要是穿上一年不走样、不开线，我给你十卢布工钱。”

谢苗害怕了，不知道怎样回答。他回头瞧瞧米哈伊尔，用手肘推推他，低声问：“接不接？”

米哈伊尔点点头，说：“接。”

谢苗听了米哈伊尔的话，同意做一双一年不走样、不开线的靴子。

老爷唤来跟班，脱下左脚的靴子，伸直腿。

“给我量尺寸！”

谢苗缝了一个十俄寸[1]长的纸样，把它抚平，又跪下来，在围裙上仔细擦了擦手，以免弄脏老爷的袜子，这才动手量尺寸。谢苗量了鞋底，量了脚背，再量小腿肚，可是纸不够大。他的小腿肚粗得像圆木。

“注意，靴筒不要做得太紧。”

谢苗又缝了一个纸样。老爷坐着，动动穿着袜子的脚趾，环顾屋里的人。他看见米哈伊尔。

“这人是谁啊？”他问。

“他是我这里的师傅，靴子由他给您做。”

“留神啊，”老爷对米哈伊尔说，“记住，要一年穿不坏。”

谢苗回头看了看米哈伊尔，看见米哈伊尔根本不瞧老爷，却盯着老爷后面的角落，仿佛盯着什么人。米哈伊尔望着，望着，突然微微一笑，容光焕发。

“傻瓜，你龇牙咧嘴干什么？你还是留点儿神，到时候把靴子做好。”

1. 一俄寸合 4.44 厘米。

米哈伊尔说："到时候一定做好。"

"那就对了。"

老爷穿上靴子，掩上皮袄，向门口走去。他忘了弯弯腰，头在门楣上撞了一下。

老爷破口大骂，摸摸脑袋，坐上雪橇走了。

老爷走后，谢苗说："哼，这可是个人物。这样的汉子棍子也打不倒。门楣都快被他撞倒了，可他却没有事。"

玛特廖娜说："过这样的日子怎么会不胖！这样的树墩连死神也搬不动。"

七

谢苗对米哈伊尔说："活儿是接下来了，我们可别给自己惹麻烦。皮子很贵，老爷脾气又大，可不能出岔子。你来吧，你眼睛尖，手艺比我强。这是尺寸，你来裁，我来上靴头。"

米哈伊尔听从他的话，拿起老爷的皮子摊在桌上，折成两半，拿起剪刀动手裁剪。

玛特廖娜走过来，看米哈伊尔裁皮子，对他的裁法

感到惊讶。玛特廖娜看惯鞋匠活儿，现在看见米哈伊尔不按鞋匠的规矩裁，而是剪成圆形。

玛特廖娜想说但没有说出来：“看来是我不懂怎样给老爷做靴子。米哈伊尔一定更懂行，我还是不要去干涉他。”

米哈伊尔裁好一双，拿起麻线缝，但不像一般做靴子那样用两根线，而是像做便鞋那样只用一根线。

玛特廖娜看见这情景感到奇怪，但还是没说什么。米哈伊尔则一直缝下去。到吃午饭的时候，谢苗站起来，看见米哈伊尔已用老爷的皮子做了一双便鞋。

谢苗大吃一惊。他想：“这是怎么搞的，米哈伊尔来了整整一年，还从未出过岔子，这回竟会闯下这样大的祸？老爷要做一双有延条的皮靴，他却做了一双不打底的便鞋，把皮子都糟蹋了。如今叫我怎样向老爷交代？这样的皮子上哪儿去找啊？”

他对米哈伊尔说：“朋友，你这是怎么啦？你这是要我的命！老爷定的是一双靴子，可你做了什么？”

他刚在责备米哈伊尔，门环响了起来，有人敲门。他们往窗外一看，看见一个人骑马跑来，正在系马。他们开了门，进来的是老爷的跟班。

“你们好！”

“你好！你有什么事？”

“太太派我来取靴子。”

“什么靴子？”

“靴子嘛！我家老爷已用不着靴子了。他归天了。”

“你说什么？”

“他离开你们，还没到家就死在雪橇上。雪橇一到家，我们要扶他下雪橇，可他已像口袋那样倒在雪橇里。他已经死了，身子都硬了。我们好不容易才把他抬下雪橇。太太就派我到这儿来。她说：‘你对鞋匠说，老爷向你们定了一双靴子，还留下皮子，现在他不要靴子了，你赶快拿皮子给他做一双死人穿的便鞋。’她还叫我等着，等你们一做好就把鞋带回家。所以我来了。”

米哈伊尔捡起桌上裁剩的皮料卷起来，拿起两只做好的便鞋拍了一下，又用围裙擦了擦，交给跟班。

跟班接过便鞋说：“再见，老板！祝你好运！”

八

又过了一年，两年……米哈伊尔住在谢苗家不觉已

是第六个年头了。他还是那样过日子，哪儿也不去，多余的话一句也不说，脸上只出现过两次笑容：一次是女主人第一回请他吃晚饭，另一次是那个老爷来定靴子。谢苗对他这个工人真是再满意不过了。他不再问他从哪儿来，只担心他离开他们。

有一天，他们都在家。女主人正把锅子放在灶上，孩子们在长凳上嬉戏，眼睛望着窗外。谢苗在一个窗口里钉靴子，米哈伊尔在另一个窗口里钉鞋跟。

一个男孩儿从长凳上跑到米哈伊尔旁边，靠在他肩上，眼睛望着窗外。

“米哈伊尔叔叔，你瞧，老板娘带着几个姑娘到我们家来了。有一个姑娘是瘸子。”

男孩儿一说完这话，米哈伊尔就扔下活儿，转身往街上望。

谢苗感到奇怪。米哈伊尔一向不往街上望，现在却伏在窗口望着什么。谢苗也往窗外望了望，果然有一个女人向他家走来，衣服干干净净，手里拉着两个身穿皮袄、头包羊毛围巾的女孩儿。两个女孩儿长得一模一样，叫你没法儿分辨，只是一个女孩儿左腿有毛病，走路一瘸一拐的。

那女人上了台阶，走进门廊，摸到门，抓住把手，打开门。她让两个女孩儿走在前头，自己跟着走进屋里。

“你好，老板！”

“请进。有什么事啊？”

那女人在桌旁坐下。两个女孩儿伏在她的膝上，她们看到陌生人有点儿害怕。

“想给这两个姑娘做两双春天穿的皮鞋。”

“行，没问题。我们没有做过这样小的鞋，但我们能做。有延条的，没延条的，都行。我们这位米哈伊尔师傅手艺可好啦。”

谢苗回头望了望米哈伊尔，看见他放下活计坐在那里，眼睛盯住两个小姑娘。

谢苗觉得米哈伊尔很怪。他想，这两个姑娘确实长得不错：黑眼睛，红脸颊，胖鼓鼓的，她们身上的皮大衣也挺漂亮。但谢苗不明白，米哈伊尔为什么这样盯着她们，仿佛认识她们似的。

谢苗感到困惑不解。他同那女人讲价钱，讲好价钱，动手量尺寸。女人把瘸腿的女孩儿抱到膝上，说：“你替这姑娘量两个尺寸；给这只跛脚做一只鞋，给这只好脚做三只鞋。她们俩的脚一样大。她们是双胞胎。”

谢苗量了尺寸，指着瘸腿的姑娘说：“她怎么会弄成这样？这么好看的姑娘。生下来就是这样的吗？”

“不，是她母亲把她压坏的。”

玛特廖娜想知道那女人是谁，姑娘们又是谁的孩子，就问：“那你不是她们的母亲吗？”

“老板娘，我不是她们的母亲，也不是亲戚，我完全是外人，只是领养了她们。”

“她们不是你自己的孩子，你却这样疼她们。”

“我怎能不疼她们呢？是我用自己的奶把她们喂大的。我自己有过一个孩子，可是上帝把他召去了，我疼他还不如疼她们呢。”

“那她们到底是谁的孩子啊？”

九

那女人就把事情从头到尾讲了一遍：

“大概六七年前吧，她们的父母在一个星期里相继去世。星期二刚葬了父亲，星期五母亲也死了。父亲在这两个孤儿出世前三天就死了，母亲生下她们连一天也没有活满。当时我跟丈夫住在乡下种庄稼，跟他们是邻

居，两家门挨着门。她们的父亲一个人在树林里干活儿。那一天一棵树倒下来，把他拦腰压住，内脏都压了出来。他被抬到家里，就把灵魂交给了上帝。他老婆就在那个星期生下双胞胎，就是这两个姑娘。贫穷，孤独，上无老，下无小。她孤独地生下孩子，孤独地死去。

“第二天早晨我去看望邻居，走进小屋，她这个可怜人已经僵了。她死的时候身子把这个姑娘压住。她就这样把她的一条腿压坏了。乡亲们走来，把她洗干净，换上衣服，装进棺材，把她埋了。都是好人帮的忙。只留下两个没爹没娘的娃娃。怎么办？当时村里只有我一人奶娃娃，我正在喂养我那才八个星期的头生儿。我就把她们暂时带回家。庄稼人聚在一起，反复商量拿她们怎么办。他们对我说：‘玛丽亚，你先把这两个娃娃带回家去，我们再想想办法。’我用奶先喂没病的那个娃娃，却不喂腿被压坏的娃娃，我想她恐怕活不成了。但后来又想，怎么能亏待那个小东西呢？我也可怜她，我就一人喂三个——自己的一个再加上这两个！我当时年轻力壮，吃得又好。上帝开恩，奶汁多得直往外流。我常常同时喂两个，让第三个等着。等两个喂饱了，再喂第三个。上帝保佑，我把这两个喂大了，可自己那一个不满两岁

就死了。上帝从此没再给我孩子，不过我们的日子越过越宽裕。现在，我丈夫在磨坊干活儿，工钱多，日子过得挺好，可我们没有自己的孩子。要是没有这两个姑娘，我真不知道日子怎么过！叫我怎能不疼她们呢？她们是我的心头肉！”

女人一手搂住瘸腿的姑娘，一手擦着脸上的眼泪。

玛特廖娜叹了口气，说：“常言说得好，没有爹娘还能过，没有上帝无法活。”

她们这样谈了一会儿，那女人站起来走了。主人两口子送她走，又回头望望米哈伊尔，只见米哈伊尔双手放在膝盖上，仰天微笑着。

十

谢苗走到他跟前说：“米哈伊尔，你怎么啦？”

米哈伊尔从长凳上站起来，放下活计，解下围裙，向主人两口子鞠躬说：“当家的，请你们饶恕我。上帝已经饶恕了我，你们也饶恕我吧。”

主人两口子看见米哈伊尔身上发出一道光。谢苗站起来，向米哈伊尔鞠了一躬说：“米哈伊尔，我知道你不

是一个凡人，我不能留你，我也不能盘问你。只是请你告诉我：为什么当我发现你，把你领回家时，你神情忧郁，等我老婆给你端来了晚饭，你对她一笑，从此你就变得高兴了？为什么后来老爷来定做靴子，你又笑了一次，而且从此变得更开心？现在，那女人带了两个姑娘来，你第三次笑了，而且容光焕发，精神振奋。告诉我，米哈伊尔，为什么你身上会发光，而且笑了三次？”

米哈伊尔回答说：“我身上发光，那是因为上帝惩罚我，如今上帝饶恕我了。我笑了三次，因为我必须懂得上帝的三个道理，现在都懂了。那天你妻子可怜我，我懂得了第一个道理，因此第一次笑了。后来富人来定做靴子，我懂得了第二个道理，因此第二次笑了。现在我看见两个姑娘，我懂得了第三个道理，也就是最后一个道理，因此第三次笑了。”

谢苗又问：“告诉我，米哈伊尔，上帝为什么要惩罚你，上帝的那三个道理是什么。”

米哈伊尔说：“上帝惩罚我，因为我不听他的话。我原是天上的天使，但我不听上帝的旨意。

“我本是天上的天使，上帝派我去勾一个女人的魂。我降到地上，看见一个女人生病躺在床上，她一胎生了

两个女孩儿。两个娃娃在母亲身旁蠕动，但她没有力气把她们抱过来喂奶。那女人看见我，知道是上帝派来取她的魂的，就哭诉道：‘天使啊！我的丈夫刚刚落葬，是被一棵树压死的。我没有姐妹，没有姨妈，没有婆婆，没人帮我养孩子。你先别取我的魂，让我先把两个孩子喂养长大！孩子没爹没娘活不成！’我听了她的话，把一个娃娃放在她怀里吃奶，另一个让她搂着，自己回到天上。我飞到上帝面前说：‘我不能取走产妇的灵魂。她男人被树压死了，她自己生了双胞胎，恳求我不要取走她的灵魂，说让她把孩子喂养长大，孩子没爹没娘活不成。我就没有取走产妇的灵魂。’上帝就说：‘你再去取那产妇的灵魂，并且弄懂三个道理：第一，人心里存在着什么；第二，人天生缺少什么；第三，人靠什么生活。等你弄懂了这三个道理，你就回天上来。’我又降到地上，取走了产妇的灵魂。

“两个娃娃就离开奶头。死人横在床上，压住了一个娃娃，把她的一条腿压坏了。我升到村庄上空，想把产妇的灵魂带给上帝，可是一阵风吹来把我的翅膀吹落，她的灵魂就单独去见上帝，而我就落到大路旁的地上。”

十一

谢苗和玛特廖娜这时才明白他们收留的人是谁，跟他们住在一起的人是谁，他们又惊又喜，不禁哭了起来。

天使说:“我就独自光着身子落在田野里。以前我不知道人们的贫困，不知道饥寒，这下我可成为人了。我肚子饿，身上冷，但不知道怎么办。我看见田野里有一座为上帝盖的教堂，就走到那儿，想在那里安身。教堂锁着，进不去。我坐在教堂后面避风。到了晚上，我又饿又冷，全身疼痛。忽然听见有人沿大路走来，手里拿着靴子，自言自语。我这是变人以后第一次看见一张凡人的脸，这脸使我害怕，我就转过身去。我听见这人在自言自语，盘算冬天用什么御寒，怎样养活老婆孩子。我想:‘我又饿又冷，现在来了一个人，可他只考虑怎样搞到皮袄给自己和妻子御寒，怎样弄到粮食充饥，他是不会帮助我的。’这人看见我皱起眉头，样子更加害怕，他从我身旁走过去。我绝望了。忽然我听见这人走回来。我朝他一看，简直认不出了:他的脸原来死气沉沉，如今变得生气勃勃，我从他脸上认识了上帝。他走到我跟前，给我衣服穿，把我领回家。我走进他家，一个女人

朝我们走过来，嘴里说着什么。这女人比男人更可怕，嘴里吐出一股死气，憋得我喘不过气来。她想把我赶到冰天雪地里，我知道，她要是把我赶出去，她准会死掉。她丈夫突然向她提到上帝，她的态度顿时变了。她给我们端来晚饭，眼睛瞧着我，我也看了她一眼，她身上的死气已没有了，变得生气勃勃，我又从她身上认识了上帝。

“我记起上帝的第一句话：‘人心里存在着什么。’我知道人心里存在着爱。上帝向我启示他交代的事，我感到高兴，第一次笑了。但我还没懂得另外两个道理。我不懂得人天生缺少什么，以及人靠什么生活。

“我在你们家里住了一年。有人来定做靴子，要能穿上一年不走样、不开线。我瞧了他一眼，忽然看见他背后有我的同伴死亡天使的影子。这个天使，除了我，谁也看不见，可我认识他，并且知道不等太阳落山这个富人的灵魂就会被取走。我想：‘这人要做一双可以穿上一年的靴子，却不知道自己已活不到晚上。’于是我想起了上帝说的另一句话：‘人天生缺少什么。’

“人心里存在着什么，我已知道了。现在我又知道了人缺少什么。人们不知道他们为了自己的肉体需要什么。我又一次笑了。我高兴的是因为看见了我的同伴死亡天

使，上帝又向我启示了第二个道理。

“但我还不懂得第三个道理。我还不懂得人靠什么生活。于是我继续等待上帝向我启示最后一个道理。第六年出现了双胞胎姑娘和那个女人。我认出这两个姑娘，知道她们是怎样活下来的。我当时想：‘母亲为了孩子求我不要取走她的灵魂，她说没有爹妈孩子们活不成，我相信了她的话，可是另一个女人把她们喂养长大了。’当这个女人爱惜别人的孩子并且痛哭流涕时，我从她身上看到了活生生的上帝，我懂得了人靠什么生活。我懂得上帝向我启示了最后一个道理并且饶恕了我，我就第三次笑了。”

十二

天使光着身子，全身发光，肉眼无法逼视。他说话的声音越来越响，仿佛这声音不是出自他的嘴，而是自天而降。天使说：“我知道，一切人活着不是靠自私，而是依靠爱。

“做母亲的不知道她的孩子要活下去需要的是什么。那富人不知道他究竟需要什么。谁也不知道，到傍晚他

需要活人穿的靴子，还是死人穿的便鞋。

“我变成了人，我活着不是依靠自己的打算，而是依靠一个过路人和他妻子的爱心，他们怜悯我，爱我。两个孤女能活下来，不是依靠母亲的照顾，而是依靠一个陌生女人心中的爱，她怜悯她们，爱她们。一切人活着不是依靠自己的打算，而是依靠人们心中的爱。

“以前我知道上帝赐给人们生命，要他们活在世上。现在我知道的事更多了。

“我懂得了，上帝不愿人们分开来生活，因此不向他们启示每个人单独需要什么；他要人们一起生活，因此向他们启示为了自己和为了大伙儿需要什么。

“现在我懂得了，人们以为他们活着靠自己的盘算，其实他们活着全靠爱。谁生活在爱之中，谁就生活在上帝之中，上帝就在他心里，因为上帝就是爱。”

天使对上帝唱起了赞美诗，他的歌声震动了小屋。这时房顶开了，一根火柱从地面直冲天上。谢苗夫妻和孩子们拜倒在地。天使张开背上的一对翅膀，升上天去。

等谢苗清醒过来，他的小屋又恢复了原状，屋里只有他们一家，没有一个外人。

企鹅经典：小黑书　第一辑

Penguin Little Black Classics Vol. I

01. GIOVANNI BOCCACCIO
Mrs Rosie and the Priest

02. EDGAR ALLAN POE
The Tell-Tale Heart

03. ANTON CHEKHOV
Gooseberries

04. LEO TOLSTOY
How Much Land Does a Man Need?

05. GUSTAVE FLAUBERT
A Simple Heart

06. RYUNOSUKE AKUTAGAWA
The Life of a Stupid Man

07. THOMAS HARDY
The Withered Arm

08. KENKO
A Cup of Sake Beneath the Cherry Trees

09. WILLIAM BLAKE
Tyger Tyger

10. RAINER MARIA RILKE
Letters to a Young Poet